Razor Smile

Humorous Poetry for Adults

Alan Joynson

For Rob Caffrey
Thank you for encouraging me – we
had a good laugh – I will always
remember you saying – voice of
aristocratic imbiber-
"You barstard, you're not going to
marry my daughter."

Contents

4

Introduction

Life is too serious to be taken seriously. My own interpretation of the above quote is try to see the funny side of life. Whenever possible.
The following poems are intended solely as an attempt at humour. Nothing more than that. Hopefully they are accessible to all age groups and may even lead certain readers to want to create their own comic verse. They are not written by someone with a degree or intended for analysis by those who have – a humorous poem or rhyme can improve your day and if that is achieved by any verse within these pages then that is all that matters.

The idea that words can add to the enjoyment of life has been very important to me from my early childhood in the 1950s and early 1960s in Newcastle under Lyme.
Programmes on radio were a particular source of enjoyment especially the song 'Goodness Gracious Me' by Peter Sellers and Sophia Loren was one of my favourites as well as 'The Ying Tong Song' by the Goons.
My mother was a big Spike Milligan fan and she even quoted Shakespeare to me – I distinctly remember, after I had been caught being economical with the truth, her saying forcefully,

'This above all: to thine own self be true'.

My father would sometimes bring home jokes or verse that were going round his office like these:

Daredaygo fortylorisinaro
Demarntloris demartrux
Fullacowsan ensandux

Daredaygo fortylorisinaro
Trere they go forty lorries in a row)
Demarntloris demartrux
(Them arn't lorries them are trucks)
Fullacowsan ensandux
(Full of cows and hens and ducks)

And the Lord said unto Moses,
All people shall have round noses,
Except Aaron,
And he shall have a square- un.

Other poems that I was introduced to, at this time, included 'The Daffodils' by William Wordsworth and 'Leisure' by W. H. Davies both of which I have included my own version in this collection.

On the TV was the programme 'Crackerjack' which often ended with a sketch including a song from the charts sung to alternative words. I will never forget my amazement when they sang a version of 'Bohemian Rhapsody'. Later on, as a teenager I was involved in productions of Gilbert and Sullivan operas, where I came across the patter song.

I am the very model of a modern Major-General,
I've information vegetable, animal, and mineral,

Our home didn't have many books. I remember my father going to the saleroom, a local auction and bringing home four encyclopaedias called 'The World of the Children' (out of date by twenty years) and a large dictionary in two volumes.

These were totally uninspiring except for some origami in 'The World of the Children'. There were also two volumes of 'Junior Science' which I definitely tried to read but finding the language difficult ie, the vocabulary.

Nearly everything in the house was bought at the sale room. It made sense as perfectly good items would get reused, they were cheaper and it was possible that 'hard up' families could get some cash – when the sale room costs were factored in however it probably wasn't that much.

I remember the song 'Second Hand Rose' on the radio and thinking of mum – she did object to all the second hand stuff as my father had plenty of money but was fairly mean with it. To be fair I should say that he had been 'pressurised' to marry mum when she became pregnant with me. It was expected in 1950s Britain.

However we did have a copy of 'Verse and Worse' which was a poetry collection by Arnold Silcock that had been given to my mother as a wedding present. The collection had several poems that appealed to me as a child all of which I've included on the following pages.

I vividly remember reading 'Castaway' and through the clever wording being 'led up the garden path'. This poem more than any other was my initial inspiration for writing poetry.

Castaway

He grabbed me round my slender neck,
I could not shout or scream,
He carried me into his room
Where we could not be seen;
He tore away my flimsy wrap
And gazed upon my form
I was so cold and still and damp,
While he was wet and warm.
His feverish mouth he pressed to mine
– I let him have his way
He drained me of my very self,
I could not say him nay.
He made me what I am.
Alas! That's why you find me here...
A broken vessel, broken glass,
That once held bottled Beer.

To see my other favourites go to page 205
and if your child wishes to have a copy feel
free to do this as there are no copyright issues.

Paws for thought

Lodercobblers

The poem below was read out on National Poetry Day 2022 at Atherstone library.

The Rude Librarian

(He'd had a REALLY BAD day, his wife had left him, the cats had both been sick on the Persian carpet the auditors were due in 12 hours and he knew he might end up in court – so when his phone rang .....)

It was three in the morning
when the phone went off
so he picked up, yawning
the librarian said 'WHAT?'

An old lady said 'When
does the library open again?'
He said 'Not 'til ten
Why would you need
To get in before then?'

(And that times about
When she started to shout)
'I don't want to get in
I want to get out.'

Hisryaterseblock

Victor Hugo often worked in the nude
(For want of a rhyme - not in Highbury)
He didn't find it at all rude
But he's banned from Atherstone library.

Shopping list

My trouble is with bad breath
So I'll watch out for a chemist
Spending fortunes at a limit
Paying hand over wrist.

We need some hens eggs
Though not hatching a plot
(Besides my allotment)
And my whistle needs a new pea.

The roof mender's been round
He's been up and says
We need to replace the elastic
membrane under the ridge tiles.

As aunty May is coming for the week end
I'll make some cauliflower soup
But aunt May has extra high standards
I'll need a perfect vegetable.

Now how am I going to remember all that?

**I know   - Super cauli ridge elastic
eggs pea halitosis.**

Nonclodhopper

They say that when you're in a garden,
You are much nearer to God.
But if you fall over
A big patch of clover
You'll end up much nearer the sod.

A Selection of Portraits of Birdwatchers

A Delboy twitcher Albert Ross
Who views the birds at Charring Cross,
And earns his cash by selling meat
He's come by slyly on the street.

A business that he's always ran,
And traded from a reliant van,
The thing that in the local bar
Was referred to as his 'butchery car.'

A cleric twitcher Rev. Kitti Wake
Was often seen out by the lake,
With her binoculars in hand
Taking in this verdant land.

She looks and scans the old church tower
Seeking for an avian bower,
She sees upon a narrow ledge
A juvenile about to fledge.

The parent lean windswept, blown
Sits by the crucifix of stone.
The birds are svelte. the church is grey.
They are of course all birds of pray.

The aged twitcher Colonel Pheasant
Doesn't help, he isn't pleasant,
So he berates the local youth
With what he thinks is gospel truth.

'Get your hair cut,' raises a titter.
'Don't snipe,' retorts the local vicar.
The youths' reply
'Bet he keeps his teeth in a night jar,'
'And if we harass him
He'll have one of his little turns.'

The Colonel, hearing this, isn't chuffed,
Doesn't rail as he's verbally cuffed
He simply says ' Owl see about that!'
And keeps his hair on. doesn't grouse.

The sixty's twitcher Randy Coot,
Who cranes his neck – the 'grand old fruit',
He'll hang about and always try,
To goose the girls as they pass by.

He swans around ducking and diving
(His battered sports car isn't thriving,)
He isn't swift at making lobby
And hasn't got another hobby.

Well there's a clutch of eccentric twitchers
Donning p'lovers unlike strippers,
And if grebious bodily harm is nigh,
Just throstle back and give a sigh,

Don't rail at them behaving oddly,
Just crow at their perplexing hobby.

Callaspade

You are nearer to god in a garden centre
Unless you're on astroturf.
And the gross superfluidties
Of hort'cultural commodities
Are three times the price that they're worth.

The items for sale are profuse
Although many are of little use;
You can buy noxious candles
Absurdly thin sandals
And even a pair of pyjamas.
You can pamper your poodle
And score apfelstrudel.
Then lift from a pocket
A lock or a socket
And then go bananas
by investing a grand
in a tank of piranhas.

But the very placenta
Of the said pay cheque render
Is the bistro that's miles from the dirt.
And if you've a spare thirty
('What get my hands dirty?!)
Join the lax status quo
To indulge and not grow
And just sit around and dodge work.

Ticketitus

A policeman pulls over a speeding car
And says,
'I clocked you doing 80 miles an hour.'
'Well officer,' the driver replies
'I'll tell the truth and not disguise
The fact I'd set the cruise control at sixty
And believe me I'm not celebrating
But perhaps your gun needs calibrating?'

In the passenger seat the wife
Who has a tongue as sharp as any knife Says,
'Listen, for on a number of occasions to me you've
made it very clear
this car has no cruise control dear.'

And as the officer writes out the ticket
And the driver thinks where he can stick it The
driver leans over to the wife and with a growl
He spews out a put down – something foul.

But the wife demurely smiles
and with wicked fire says,
'Well your speed could have been even higher,
Be thankful for your little protector
You know, your handy radar detector.'
As the officer writes out another note
The driver says
'I'll ram that tongue right down your throat,' but
the policeman who is now staring, says,

'I notice sir that you're not wearing
A seat belt (an oft committed crime)
And that's an automatic fine.'

The driver now of a less confident mind
Says, 'Well I had it on my shoulder
But seeing you coming over
I slipped it off its clip and sprocket,
So I could get my licence out o'my back pocket.'
The wife now speaks, she shows no fear,
she says
'But you never wear your seat belt dear.'
The driver now can hardly breathe,
His very being starts to seethe,
His face now a purplish hue,
He says ' Be quiet or I'll murder you!'
The officer says
'Does your husband always talk to you this way
ma'am?'
Thinking –'The road hog's crap at keeping calm!'
Says she,
'I can see the way you're thinking
But no, ... well ....
Only when he's been drinking.'

Aquabatic

In my first swimming lesson said Zack–
'Dad threw me in pushing my back.
The Thames water shook me
And I found that it took me
Ten minutes to get out of the sack!

17

Petalpower

An accident happened to my sister Dot
When down came a daffodil from a high spot –
Now flowers are harmless but this one was not,
It came sweetly scented and wrapped in a pot.

Legerdemand

The goblins ran a factory to manufacture spells,
And went recruiting fairies
from the local woodland dells.
But conditions in the factory
they were not up to scratch,
A loud explosion blew out three
when someone lit a match.
Chorus
So, lets call the elfen safety
and keep the workplace bright,
Lets call the elfen safety,
when all we need's a light.

The goblins on the management
they tried to up the pace,
Since a lot of time the pixies spent
just staring into space.

The cold it stopped them flying
Which the fairies didn't like,
So then the pixie union
went out and called a strike.

See, we need the elfen safety,
their wonders to perform:
Yes, we need the elfen safety,
to keep the workforce warm.

The spells production method
was to use a small black hole,
Suspended over three large hobs
all filled with burning coal.

But then the fairies flying by
were sometimes sucked inside,
And so a pixie's angry cry
berated and replied.

'Oh, where's the elfen safety,
it really is a shame,
If we had elfen safety,
There'd be someone else to blame.'

Thighpriority

Two men in ASDA were chatting
One young and the other quite grey,
And neither knew where their wives were
So old Bert said 'Nick' in his way –
.'What does your lady look like?'
'Well she's blond and she wears a short
skirt
High-heels and legs that are suntanned
But what does your lady look like Bert?'
(He asked as he stood by the doors.)
'No matter,' said Bert and went on to
assert,
'Let's just go looking for yours.'

Gobalotacarp

The cause of all the trouble
His language wasn't suitable.
For he belittled her 'idea bubble'
With language - disreputable.

So when asked if he was hungry
and the answer was affirmative,
She then prepared his food
and laced it thoroughly with laxative.

Horsing Around

Crossing merry England's state,
A bishop who was ready,
To stop the coach and alleviate
His need to spend a penny.

A lonely farmhouse came in view
They stopped and asked a skivvy.
'Oh farmer, wherefore is the loo?'
'Your Lordship, it's yon privy.'

The Bishop hurried out of sight
And came back much relieved.
'My gratitude to you, it's right,
And this I have conceived;

A gold chain I will send to you
It will replace the rope I wrecked,
It is the least that I can do.'
But the farmer he looked vexed.

I am annoyed, it's got my goat,'
(Yes more than just a smidgeon,)
'I wish you hadn't pulled that rope,
You've let out all my pigeons.'

Arachnidawn

The spider
To her mind
Came like a scream
Amplified
She froze,
Then twitched
Then rigid again
Was she .....
Arachnified?

With shaking hand,
with cup and card
Her gut uit wrenched inside
It hadn't moved
What did that prove?
'Lying doggo'
She thought
No malice removed.

Forcing her arm
the cup came down
Something was wrong and useless
Nerves in a stew
At gallons of goo
Her thoughts - fruitless
But as the legs spread by the bin
with the bread.
She realised.
All along the spider
had been
dead.

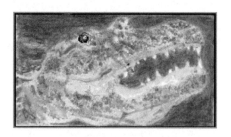

Bellocking

If your bank account is emptied
And to speed a legacy you're tempted
To do away your sleeping mater
By use of hungry alligator

Yes if earthly greed does get to you
Then they will surely come for you
They'll an'lyse that you try to hide
And bring a charge of mattresside.

They'll come with drug and lie detector
And probe your inner Thalamic centre.
They'll know you think like Roman traitor
That you're very glad he ate her.

Or if you're tempted poison wise,
Like henbane with your silicide.
They can trace a valence pattern
Down to the lowly single atom.

But if your success in lawlessness
Means you and Pa will tour Loch Ness.
The press will call you 'Greedy Cuss'
Who got one up on Oedipus.

Youjuice

Twas an evening in September
As I very well remember,
I was walking in the jungle with my guide. When a
shriek yelled by some nutter
Made my heart go all a flutter,
And a cannibal appeared, right by my side.

Yes. I stood there (I'll not stutter)
Thinking thoughts of m..m..me with butter When
my wife with pointing gun did loudly say,
'You can tell that this defuses
When a club is all he uses'
At that the cannibal just walked away.

Appropriate Memorial Trees

Internet obsessed.	Apple
Jilted lover.	Sycamore
Batsman.	Willow
Baker.	Breadfruit
Heavy Smoker.	Ash
Policeman	Copper Beech
Coastal Lifesaver.	Beech
Isle of Man flogger.	Birch
Amazon obsessed.	Box
Ship steersman.	Elm
Toothless man.	Gum
Aggressive equine.	Horse Chestnut

24

Playing Fliszt

The Royal College of Music library
For scores that I can teach
Is perfect, and fully sedentary
That's where I Haydn seek.

The Germans they're represented here
With works of sheer delight
Schutz and Schein we do revere
And sev'ral works by Scheidt.

And there for all our canine friends
Some scores of music's art
And my own dog his voice will lend
He'll whine and Offenbach

For some the mention of JS Bach
Their praise is automatic
And some believe, he practised on
A virginal in the attic.

The story goes....
A new arrival in Australia, possibly someone sentenced to transportation, saw one of these creatures and asked an aborigine the name of the animal, to which the aborigine replied 'Kangaroo' – which in his language meant 'I have no idea what you're asking me.'

The Wonders of the Miniverse

Hippex

With life it's hard to get to grips
And work at my relationships,
But Aunties now have tripped on stones
And damaged fragile pelvic bones,
So cares I have (and things to fix)
As well as my relations' hips.

In   herr   it

On social-distancing
My commiserations
It's hardly conducive
To human relations
But such as my fam'ly
(Of rank infestations)
Have perfected the art now
For whole generations.

Literally a Princess

The consummate works of Jane Austin
Those novels that readers get lost in.
Her Stoke on Trent style beats Dahl by a mile,
With insight and judgement are bostin'.

Walletoutitus

Mental health problems had Jock
The tight-fisted Scot,
Who went by the surname of Jammening
And he yelled 'If you think
I'd pay for a shrink
Why if I did I'd need my head examining.

Sober Judge Meant

A dame wed a hack a New Yorker
Her spouse ailed and debt it soon caught her.
She took up beer brewing
That got five star reviewing
And made porter support her reporter.

Grotisnort

Never pinch a bison's nose
While vets deal with a tumour
Untranquilised - each ranger knows
He has no sense of humour.

Yeeeeeeeeeeeeeeees

I'll state my opinion in unique verse
On the two things that stretch to infinity.
The first is the size of the universe
The other is man's stupidity.

Poem to the Great Unwashed

Without a shower,
I'm saving power
And cash and time he thinks,
But I've been near him
And had to breathe in
So I say I don't care what he thinks
It's really a case of ....

.

Evil to him who evil stinks!

Idigthat

A Thai Mozart fanatic Doh Zing
Opened Mozarts' grave exposing
Him working sans pause
To cross out his scores
It seems he was still decomposing.

From Bard to Vorse

By any other name a rose
as sweet would smell
And by any other name
a rhododendron
would be easier to spell.

Ornymusing

To be informedis my pursuit
For the Scots' they differ a moorhen and coot.

A coot if you've bad luck saves a splash from a
truck.
And a moorhen is always more hen than duck.

Spud I's

I counted the eyes on my potatoes
Before they sat up by the leeks
I needed a rough guide
Had I enough supplied
To see me through the week?

Mobzombie

Moving up the pavement
Wearing loud headphones
Crossing roads as day went
Mind the traffic cones!
Your steps seem automatic
But to accident you're prone
How can you see the traffic
WHEN YOU'RE STARING AT YOUR PHONE!

Thinnerick

Whilst slimming a young girl Evette
Lost weight by much more than was set,
She said she was glad to,
But found that she had to,
Run round in the shower to get wet.

Loingirder

Not a very funny bird is the peregrine,
His face will never be a merry grin.
Running fast you will see his eyes a glower,
If you can run at 200 miles-an-hour!

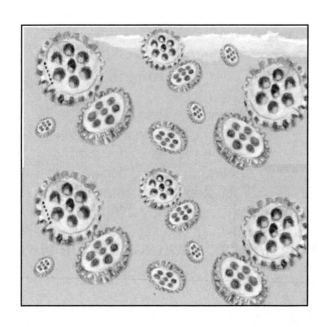

Toretion

Bill he needed gearbox parts
For the motor that he ran,
But none were here so to make a start
He flew them from Japan.

But over Wales the plane broke up
And car parts fell in wads,
And a local wag he said 'Oh look,
It's raining Datsun cogs.'

Scullerymade

I view the sliced beetroot that stains
The lino near the kitchen door.
Consuming the remaining gains
And now I'm red in tooth and floor.

Dinequiner

A stable relationship
I decided upon.
She looks like a horse
And I eat like one.

Winceanblue

The newly released prisoner
realised that the friendliest people
were sometimes to be found
behind bars.

Meteorcareerad

The advert for the new human cannon ball
Brought so many they couldn't count em all,
They were auditioned by the Circus Excalibur
But no one was found of the requisite calibre.

Out-Clapped

And have you heard about the retired–
Italian opera singer's dilapidated Vauxhall –
She calls it her Caverlieria Rusticana.

The Englishman   An Australian jest.

Q, Where does an Englishman hide his money?
A. Under the soap.

Needapasting?

You must never wade in a high risk glue
It's a quite in adhesivable thing to do,
But should ignore my tactless conclusion
Don't fail to find the most diluted solution.
(With apologies to Spike Milligan)

Agonorea

Roy bought a brand new hearing aid,
He said this to his friend –
'The old one it was not well made,
Fell in the toilet last week end.

We got a new one - it cost a bit
The wife even said 'I agree."
Roy's friend said 'Really, what kind is it?'
Roy answered 'Half past three.'

Hermindset

Sue tried on a tight dress she thought dated
And asked her two friends how they'd rate it.
Her pals gave a snort
'Too expensive, too short,'
Asphyxiated she wheezed, 'I'll take it.'

Maleveto

Bigamy may be a case,
Of two rites making a wrong,
but it's usually having
one husband too many-
Like monogamy, claims Erica Jong.

Irelandfling

When words I seek to sketch my wife
I think of grouse and duck.
For near me on the wall may strike
Some tea and then the cup!

She says I never listen to her
Or something a bit like that
And if I grouse, her ire will stir
And then she'll throw the cat.

Her knowledge vast you can forget
Those icloud mem'ry banks,
And if I whisper 'know all' I will get
A cauliflower ear for thanks!

Riverthick

Cleopatra believed that the Nile
Contained a benign crocodile,
She went for a swim
Was torn limb from limb,
And her spirit is still in denial.

Meantimes

A new light bulb he thought a high cost consequence
Which showed his home maintenance incompetence
So the hole in the floor
Behind the attic door
Meant he fell knowing regular incontinence.

Multineedling

At 80 miles per hour
A patrol car pulled alongside,
An old lady whose elbows
Were to steering applied.

Her hands they were knitting,
And windows open wide-
The policemen yelled, **'Pull Over!'**
'No socks,' she replied.

Fangs for the Memory

If Dracula's trailing your wife-
There's bound to be a disturbance.
And beware if he offers eternal life
He's not trying to sell you insurance.

Pater-retaP

He came from a family of talented acrobats so
naturally his father was an excellent role model.

Insanouts

I phoned a bloke to play cricket
But his wife said 'You're out of luck
He's gone poaching along with Al Trillwick'
So without playing he was 'out for a duck.'

Sofarasitgoes

We all know you can't make an omelette
Without the breaking of eggs,
Or run in a marathon and not get
Away without two aching legs.

Nolaughmatter

A notice was found on the church floor,
Now pinned on the board and we saw,
'Please would Miss Stoop
and the Low Esteem Group,
Remember to use the back door.'

Getitaff

Here lies Jean Wright,
She was killed by a fright.
Her name was not Wright but Wheel,
But Wheel would not rhyme with fright
But Wheel's right.

Brownedoff

At the home of old Richard Tomarlows
He has roses he's grown from two car loads.
Even where his wife Jude,
Sunbathes in the nude,
Which is odd as he planted tomatoes.

Deaquefied

An indian from the old wild west
Was riding on a train.
His name was 'Big Chief Stanting Bull'
His squaw was 'Little Flame.'

He sent his squaw to fetch a drink
Three times it all befell,
On third return she said, 'Me can't,
Um paleface sitting on well."

Appropriate Remembrance Trees

Fortune teller	Palm
Tramp's mutt.	Pawpaw
Dumped Paramore.	Pine
English geologist.	Pomegranate
Well liked bloke.	Poplar
Arboreal analyst.	Redwood
Desertwelly designer	Sandalwood

Cumminpuffin?.

Puffin mating for twitchers is thrilling
They may rub beaks it's called 'billing',
The male's also got
A march on the spot,
But what matters the most - is she willing?

Who'dbeawaiter?

The waiter was with Ma'am Clearage
When the creme brulee fell down her cleavage.
He warmed up a spoon
She squawked 'STOP YOU BUFFOON!
It might thwart my assent to the peerage.'

Pointaken

After - dinner speeches we all have to bear
Are like a bull's horns in an arena
There's a point here, there's a point there
With an awful lot of bull inbetweena.

Frugivor

A bird that's unique is the toucan
And in some ways it compares to a human
For fruit eater it's classed
Though its inputs so vast
One man can't compete,
No but two can.

Idigthat

A Thai Mozart fanatic Doh Zing,
Opened Mozart's grave exposing,
Him working without pause,
To cross out his scores,
It seems he was still decomposing.

1960s - Marriage – a woman's view?

It starts when you fall for his charms
And then you sink into his arms,
But alarms are set off as you think
'It will end-up with my arms in his sink.'

Cumulovision

I'd never drive at a purple ewe
Especially with my specs on.
For then I'd see a double ewe
And ram my misconception.

Oooooooooouch!

A heinous sex tourist named Horrocks,
Was took hostage whilst crossing the Trossacks,
His captors - (minds twisted)
They simply enlisted,
A sniper who shot off his b.........

Zany Views

Short notes on pets that can perform simple household tasks

How useful it would be if
As well as the obvious benefits
Your cat could say- do the ironing.
Or the budgie could post a letter.
I'd prefer a ferret that could clean your car. You
know he'd be able to reach all those parts the
vacuum couldn't.
Or even a rabbit that that did the dusting. Dogs
would of course feature highly in this
As their benevolent nature
and innate intelligence would suit them to many
tasks,
Such as cleaning the windows or making soup.
The male dogs might prefer the manly jobs like
mowing the lawn or mending a window. And the
house-proud bitches could do the washing up,
But that's entirely up to them.
I wouldn't insist... and I'd do things for them in
return
Like throwing a stick or buying a tin of food,
We'd just be helping one another.

(Dedicated to the radio 3 programme 'The Verb' and particularly the
voice of Ian Macmillan)

Snogger

Ewan kissed me by the spring
And Bernard by the pool,
And Lenny thinks I'll wear his ring!
(He must think I'm a fool.)

I'll kiss Tom whose lousy cold
To me to germs exposes,
But Mark is camp and wet and old
And he has halitosis.

I've kissed some very handsome men
Like Mick who comes from Wick,
But if Martin kisses me again
I think that I'll be sic

Voodooitall

In public loo a doctor sat
Wishing cures for cancers
But he smiled when he saw
Scribed low on the door
'Beware of limbo dancers

Denilebattle

The boy stood on the burning deck,
Whence all were in retreat,
His bloodshot eyes were filled with tears
His shoes were filled with feet.

Then up and spake our Captain Bold
Oh good lad have a care.'
But Captain Bold, his heart was cold,
He'd lost his teddy bear.

The boy still stood though abandon ship
Was called out on the wreck,
But no one had a clue his shoes,
Were glued on to the deck.

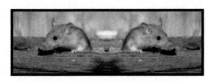

Then fifty rats jumped from below
Came tumbling on the deck,
And sailors all did hear their call
'We're out of 'ere, by heck!'

Now the captain grabbed the lad
And pulls him by the ear,
And they escape the burning place
The sailors they all cheer.

Now fighting wars is quite insane
And stupid we'd agree,
Real WAR? No thanks! it was a game,
We're playing on TV.

The boy was on the burning deck,
The pride of all the fleet.
His weary eyes now show surprise
And he still has his feet.

Dearjohn

A lonely farmer
A wife he lacked her
Met Sue so all thought
When would he ask her?

Folks watched and were keen
While he covered his machine
With garlands he'd seen
Numbered up to sixteen

It was the talk of the place
And viewing her face
Knew this was his ace
And he said it was done to attract her.

Stinginthtale

(David Attenborough voice – wasp in high
magnification fills screen)
Sideswipe Vespula Engrossopola,
Known commonly in India as the Challalii
- literally fat wasp.
Never excavates a nest below ground as..
(Wasp stings DA) Off Camera – 'Ow The little......'
(Controls voice.) .... ' do his British equivalents
or indeed raid the nests of
other smaller insects due to its
generous proportions.
It is therefore never referred to
In its native land at least as -
'Neither a burrower nor a slender bee.'

45

Huntipocrats

If swatting flies it's not much use
To don red coat on horse with bowler.
So spare us all the lame excuse
Of altruistic pest controller.

Crank Designs

The property was advertised
On an upmarket Google site,
Well positioned and secluded
Though it didn't seem quite right.

The framework of the building
Was solid beyond belief.
Though a entirely free of gilding
Which we viewed with great relief.

There was no double glazing
Or roof parts or a door.
Though the view it was amazing
And grass grew on the floor.

The local farmer's livestock could
Prefer to wander there.
And swooping from a local wood
Two barn owls came to stare.

(But we bought it because)
It really was important to
Impress our sham 'close' friends
That's why we saw the project through
To renovate Stonehenge

Crematakeyboard

When I was on line
The other day.
Visiting sites
Where you don't have to pay.
Joined in a chat room
And typed away,
But then it dawned on me
That they were all gay!
And that's why I'm about to –

Sling and torch the router
Because it will be fun
And I'll burn the computer
(Clickerty clickerty click)
And get out in the sun!

My eyes are now square
And my nerves are frayed
My backside is melded
to the chair I'm afraid
I'm an inside man
As I'm trapped in the shade
And my power point plan
Has crashed and decayed.
And that's why I'm about to;

Sling and torch the router
And give thanks when it's done
And I'll re-program the computer
(Clickerty clickerty click)
With a gun!

My waistline is growing '
Cause the fat it is storing
My blood pressure's rising
And the migraine is soaring
My mind's apoplectic
Because U-tube is boring
And you can't tell the web sites
from the carpet or flooring.
And that's why I'm about to

Sling and torch the router
For all the trouble and strife
And I'll shred the computer
(Clickerty clickerty click)
–sound effect; crunching metal
And get a life!

Heavenset

'How many clocks are on that wall**?'**
St. Peter answered ,'Lots.'
'And each one goes back an hour
When he acts like clot
'But where's the clock for 'Ronald Crump'
'Best rid of... 'snarled the man.
'Oh that ones in my office now,
I use it as a fan.'

Hair today

Young Tom at the barbers
His hair near the deck
Was an estimate needed
Or scaffolding set?

'How much d'yer want off'
asked barber O'Syd?
Eyes closed the lad coughed–
'How much for three quid?'

He thought of a pop star
With hot-fuzz top lid
'Do it just like me father's
Just like a clown's wig'

O'Syd snipped so fast
With electric shock punch
And with the other hand rampant
In his face stuffed his lunch

Hair falling everywhere
Near six inches deep
But O'Syd'd just got going
Next up was Shaun Sheep

With countenance grimaced
Adept lawn mower care
And when he'd finished
There was still one hair there!

'Contactless' Tom paid up
Threw a small sock of coins
Which O'Syd caught back handed
But gave him strained groins

(O'Syd, wrote poetry
In a notebook he carried
'Contactless' the thought came
'Just like me being married.')

Tom rolled home through park
Like a red snooker ball
Tom thought - 'I'll get him
I'll bring dog an'all!'

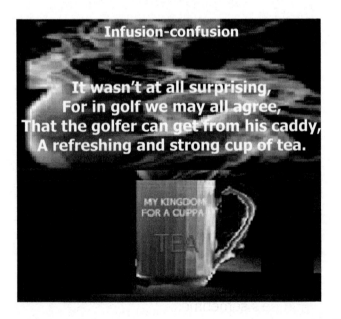

Infusion-confusion

It wasn't at all surprising,
For in golf we may all agree,
That the golfer can get from his caddy,
A refreshing and strong cup of tea.

MY KINGDOM
FOR A CUPPA

TEA

Three characters whose pub-lodgers of
remarkable
consistency

Amnesiboozer

Forgive Balid Cruz,
For the fact that he does,
Drink lager and wine by the flagon.
For I've heard on my phone,
He has problems at home,
And his wife, it is known, is a dragon.

Imbiberess

And forgive Maxis Crewe,
As actors will do,
Drinks absinthe
and often gets plastered.
Her life's not enriched,
As pregnant she hitched,
To a man, who's a word,
I've not mastered.

Dodgeredo

And then there's old Pap,
Who's seen with his cap,
In the pub, as he sits, on his throne.
He's full of good cheer,
As he swigs at his beer,
And he's sometimes been known to go home.

'You think it's bad in here,
just wait 'til you get outside –
they bash your head in!'

Lieder Here

Cock-up Cook

And now the end is near
And so I face the final sturgeon
My friend there was that year
I cooked a skate for Richard Burton.

I've made a raspberry fool
And sold them on,
on Smallbrook Ringway
And more, much more than this
I worked at Fryways.

Vinaigrettes I've made a few
But then again t'was my invention
I sliced what I had to stew
And puréed too, to get attention.
I planned each separate course
Each pukka dish
Whilst singing 'My way'
And more, much more than this
I worked at Fryways.

Yes there were times
I'm sure I knew
When they bit off
more than they could chew
But through it all
when there was trout
They ate it up and spat it out,
The boss did bawl
Back to the wall!
When I worked at Fryways.

I've peeled, I've chipped and fried,
The dishes were not of my choosing
And now the boss is snide
I find it all rather bruising.
To think I cooked all that
And may I say not in a Thai way
Oh no, not Starbucks me
I worked at Fryways.

For what is a flan what it got?
If not a crust then we has must not
Just add the things it truly needs
And not to mind the way it feels
But the record shows my flans had holes
When I worked at Fryways. ...

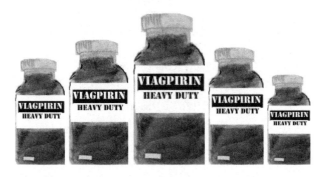

*(An elderly professor of chemistry sits in his laboratory
and as a distraction from some of his murderous
thoughts, he is changing labels on jars in an attempt to
conceal the amounts of poison he will later steal with the
motive of poisoning his wife, Dove, because she bullies
and humiliates him in public. He is also mildly infatuated
with a good looking laboratory assistant, Meg.*

Labels

I sit here late
Does a label complicate my life?
And does she know
The places where they go?
Now I'm grey and old,
Cause I haven't been told,
That cessations in my mind unfold,
So when I'm lying in my head,
Thoughts running through to Meg
And I wish that Dove was dead.
I'm moving labels instead.

But through it all she hammers me correction,
And not of love and affection,
Whether I'm bright or strong,
And Dove I'll slaughter, fall,
However it may shake me
I know that she wont break me,
When she comes to maul,
she wont placate me.
I'm moving labels instead.

When I'm feeling bleak,
And the stain moves up a one layer sheet
I hook above,
And I know I'll always be vexed with Dove
And now the feeling grows,
She'll wreak flesh from my bones
And when Dove is dead
(shakes head – he clearly does not want to kill her)
I'm moving labels instead.

But through it all she hammers me correction
And not of love and affection
Whether I'm bright or strong
And Dove I'll slaughter, fall,
However it may shake me
I know that she won't break me,
When she comes to maul,
she won't placate me.

Grimly Suppressed

Don't call me I won't need you
If my house was on fire.
Don't come to me
Go from me your time has expired.
So you're here with me,
That is all I don't need.

It's 'get a life' time.
Your promises are of a wimp that screams.
You speak the language of love
Like <u>you</u> know what it means.
Mm and your always wrong
Take my car and stray a long way.

You're simply a pest
Wetter than all the rest
Bettered by anyone
Anyone who's ever wet

I'm struck when you start,
You bang on over words I say,
Keep us apart really
You will rather be dead.

You depart so jumps my heart
at every night and day.
If you're wise you'll get lost
Just get washed away.
S'long as I'm not in your arms
Just hear these words in your face.

You're simply a jest
Lesser than all the rest
Glibber than anyone
I'M WISHING I HAD NEVER MET.

*Paula Sherpa on a TV Cooking Show mistakenly believes she
is ahead, whilst also seeing her failure unfolding, as her new
recipe Dove Suzette slowly congeals, when she decides that
duck would have been a better option. Cher your views.*

Anthem to Doomed Cooking

When you're clearly
Steaming pork.
When meat has filled your pies
I will try them all.
Rinds on the side.

Sometimes it's tough
But keep your cool (don't frown).
Like the fridge by the puddled water
It will lay steam down.

Like the fridge by the puddled water
You may want to drown.
When it's down the spout
When you're in a stew.

When puddings sets so hard
I will laugh with you.
I'll try your tart,
When it's rock hard
And stains are all around.
Like the fridge by the cuisine altar
You may wear a crown.
Like the fridge by the cuisine altar
You will soon turn brown.

(U tube – Fridge repair man visits kitchen –
he leaves – later cook phones –
repair man returns – cook happy fridge ok –
thumbs up.)

Capon silver grill
Baste and fry.
Your wine was mixed with brine
Now it's in the sky.
See how it binds
With Tate and Lyle
And now quite soon you'll find.
Like a fridge that's a double faulter
You won't have to mind.
Like a fridge that's a double faulter
Sugar's less refined.

White Richmist

I'm dealing with a site wish-list
Just like the one I think you know,
And the interests risen,
By forecasts driven,
Will raise the overdraft I grow.
I'm dealing with a site wish list,
With ev'ry troll email I type.
May your bills at Christmas be slight,
And may all your purchases be light.

Burk Leave

No matter which lard I try
You keep gushing at my side
And I can't scrape roux
When I'm talking to you

In my sad mind I'm leading
It takes thyme (you believe it?')
But after all my dove is done
I'm going to be the empty one.

**Do you gut- grieve in life after dove
I can feel something inside me rail
I really don't think it's stroganoff No!
Do you re-heave the chyme after dove
I can feel something inside me weigh
I really don't drink it strong enough No!**

Have I not suffused for you
Bread in rounds and plate for two
Well you can screw that!
Though the toast's turning black!

You need time to roux on
I need duck to deal strong
'Now I'll have time to shrink from view
Maybe my dove's too good for you!

(An infants teacher muses over her situation and leisure time.)

Pesterday

Pests today, all my students seem to be at play,
Now I wish that they would float away,
Oh there will be no rest today.
Luckily, it's not half the hour it used to be,
But there's a target hanging over me,
End of term is near you see.
Why they are so slow
I don't know (brain cells too few?)
(holds nose)
I sense something strong
it must be on someone's shoe.

(Dreaming)
Saturday, I was shopping and I'm glad to say, That I've
sorted out my holiday,
Hiking down the Pennine Way.
(Back in classroom)
When will their minds grow,
it's as if they're made of clay.
May be wont be long now
before my hair goes grey.

Cant display, work that is already done today. When I
sleep tonight I'll lie awake.

That surely was a less hair day.
Mm mm mm mm not ok
Mm mm mm mm
pesterday!

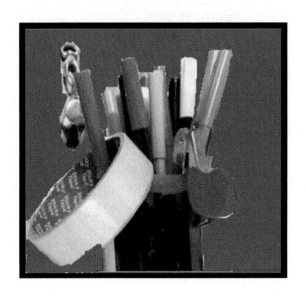

*Arnold is fanatical about his garden and is
outraged by his neighbour's cat which keeps
depositing offensive material in his
rose bed and then
spending hours basking in the sun on an old
cushion within arms reach, on the other side
of the hedge. He plans to make a device
which will replace the cushion and end his
problem.*

Cremoggymate

When the thread is drawing
Round the polyester storing,
When the charge is in there
With the three-fuse waiting for me.
Got me no TNT But I'll see to that,
Yes it won't be pretty
When I kill my neighbour's cat!

Is this the way to arm-a-pillow
Every night I've been hiding in willow,
Really seems I've armed a pillow
And sweet revenge it waits for me.
Blow me away I've armed a pillow,
I've had jeebies, I'm not mellow,
Trying covers on a pillow
I'll go and get the TNT.

Sha la la ia Ia ia ia ia (X 3) (Loud explosion)

And sweet oblivion's here for me.
There's a church bell ringing,
There's the sound of people singing Ave Maria.
Means this guy's not going to be there.
I'm beyond the skyway, Spy an open plain,
And I keep on going, Won't be back again.
It is not wise to arm a pillow,
I'm a recent departed fellow,
I wish I hadn't armed a pillow,
Should not have used the TNT.

Sha la la ia Ia ia ia ia (X 3) (Loud explosion)

Mutemanopause

For a week I've not spoken to my wife
She thinks my views corrupt.
It just makes for a quiet life
And I don't like to interrupt.

Frugivor

A bird that's unique is the toucan,
And in some ways it compares to a human,
For fruit eater it's classed
Though its inputs so vast,
One man can't compete
No but two can.

The Sound of Crew-Zips

Stain drops from noses and blisters where skin-ends
Light copper models who warm when a writ ends
Soaking wet mattresses thrown out 'til spring
These are a few of my unfavourite things

Taking your clothes off with blue static flashes.
Cars where the alarm goes off after it crashes
Tall smelly fitters that weld back the springs
These are a few of my unfavourite things.

Lean suited phonies with loud London labels
Cow bells and pay bells and pigtails on poodles
Vile wheezy actors who moon in the wings
These are a few of my unfavourite things.

When the frogs binge - when the tree sings
When I'm in Singsing,
I simply remember my unfavourite things
and then I don't feel so.......

*S/E Gun Shot

Dippa's Song

Bud beer's at 'The Spring'
And daze at the morn.
Bar-links at seven?
The Pils guide's brew-curled.
The dark's on the rim,
The pale's robbed the horn.
Grog's on 'til 'leven
All's light with the world.

(The following poem 'Boatheavian Crapsody' is based on the following story after a family argument, Mark, a wellmeaning, but incompetent teenager, is at sea in a small boat to try and catch fish to keep his mother's failing chip shop business afloat. He is phoning for the lifeboat. whilst the unfamiliar rocking of the boat is having predictable consequences.......)

65

Boatheavian Crapsody

Is this the real strife
Is this just fallacy?
Thought in my mind slides
Row, escape from normality.
(Very sea sick)
Thinking of fries
Hook up for the pies and tea.
Oh----poor joy
Because my queasy tum, eas'ly goes,
Middle high, middle low,
Anyway the wind blows really really matters to me,
to me.
Mama, just chilled a van.
'Do your best' is what she said,
Now the trigger fish is dead.

Mama the tide has just begun
And now I've gone and cast my line away.
Mama, ooh,
Always hoped to let you fry.
If I'm not back by train this time tomorrow
Carry on, carry on,
as if nothing really matters.

To date my chyme's not come.
My dinner's on my mind
Body's wretching all the time.
Flood by everybody,
I'm good to go,

I will leave it all behind and change the tune.
(Boat rocking and wind increase alarmingly)
Mama, ooh (any way my wind blows)
I want you to fry,
I sometimes wish I'd never been aboard at all.

I see a little pirouetto of a prawn
Shovelnose, Shovelnose you are not from Vendango.
(Holding small fish)

Thorneyhead and whiting
Isnt really brightening me.
(Sacramento) Sacramento! (Sacramento)
Sacramento! Sacramento Danio!
Mud minnow go!
I'm just a saw boy and somebody loves me.
He's just a saw boy from a raw family
Spare him his life from this monster of sea.

Queasy come, queasy go,
It wont let me go,
Fish killer! No, please don't make me throw
(Set him low!)
Fish killer! Please don't make me throw –
(Set him low!)
Fish killer! Please don't make me throw –
(Set him low!)
Please don't make me throw –
(Set him low!)
Please don't make me throw

(Never, never, never let me throw) Up!
Oh, Oh, Oh, Oh, Oh, Oh, No.
(Oh Mam I fear, dihorea's what I fear,
let me show Poseidon
has a weevil put aside for me,
for me, for me.)
(He becomes delirious – lifeboat on the skyline)
So you think you can clone me
and spit in my fly.

So you think you can glove me
and I'll get to try.
Oh lady, won't do this to me, lady,
Trust oughta get out,
Trust oughta get right outta here.
(Lifeboat rescues him)
(Oh yeah Oh, yeah) (Mother)

Something really matters
I hope that you can see.
It's you that really matters
(Holding up small fish caught earlier)

But nothing really batters for tea.
(Any way my wind blows.)

Blackanblue

The whispers are a warning
Of Rover's sleepy night
Are snoring deep under now
He shut eyes the sky
And he instantly wakes
I hold on to his wet body

I wished now (I remember)
I'd not saved him from that lake.

'Cause I am from Fazeley
And you are my tan
Whenever you go-for-me
I'll reach for that can

Lost and now I'm feeling
Wishing I was armed
When the dodo outside's
Too much to take
That all ends when I'm rid of you

Even though there are many times
I drive my car away
You're always howling where I am
So I wish to see you slide

'Cause I'm not O'Grady
And you are no fan
Whenever you howl at me
I'll run as fast as I can.

Gherkinhater

What did I go without and start south,
Ruddy great thing you're making me shout,
You've got my hair thinning, no kidding,
I can't pull you down.
What's going on? It's that hid'ous design.
Not at all magical. Mammonite shrine.
And I'm so queasy, I know what's hit me!!
'Cause you' re such a sight.

**My gut's under slaughter and I'm breathing
fire.
I'm crazy and I know what I'll find.**

**You're tall you see spoil all the view
Hate your curves and all your edges
All your pigeon crap and ledges**

**You're too tall for me
I wish the fall of you.**

**Not my friend and temper's thinning
And when you're down I'm grinning,
'Cause my skin all crawls on me
And I wish the fall of you. Oh oh.**

How many times have I wished wrecking crews
We could be descrying our beautiful view.
The world is shunning our town,
I'm around in every mood.
Pray my council light the fuse
The worse distraction in dustbin it's due.

Delivered by 'Zantapaws'
(with maximum packaging)
the rich-bitch branch of 'Brazilriver Inc.'

Amuseolieder

Christmas Humour

Hark, the herald angels sing,
Beecham's pills are just the thing,
They are gentle, meek and mild,
Two for an adult, one for a child
. If you want to go to heaven
You must take a dose of seven,
If you want to go to hell,
Eat the blinkin' box as well...

We three kings of Leicester square,
selling ladies underwear.
So fantastic, no elastic
Why don't you buy a pair?
O star of wonder, bright to light,
Sit on a box of dynamite!
Light the fuse and you will see
the quickest way to the cemet'ry.

Good King Wenceslas looked out
In his pink pyjamas,
Sliding down the banisters,
Eating bad bananas.
Brightly shone the moon last night
Over Marks and Spencers,
Then a Scotsman came in sight
And he knocked him senseless.

Zanydood

Yankee Doodle went to town
Riding on a pony-
He stuck a feather in his hat,
And called it macaroni.

Chorus: Yankee Doodle keep it up,
Yankee Doodle dandy,
Mind the music and the step
And with the girls be handy.

Yankee Doodle had a farm,
Where he kept cows for butter,
And hens to lay him hard boiled eggs
For breakfast lunch or supper.

Yankee Doodle likes his beer
He drinks it by the flagon.
And you could say he needs it
As his wife she is a dragon.

Yankee Doodle often tries
To find a place that's calmer.
And you may see him on the roof
While eating a banana.

Yankee Doodle stays out late
On ev'nings when it's balmy.
And now his fav'rite takeaway,
Is Chicken biriami.

(The song below was very popular at my primary school.)

Drill Ye Tarriers

Every morning at seven o'clock
There's twenty tarriers a workin' at the rock Then
the boss comes along and he says, 'Keep still
And come down heavy on the cast iron drill.'

Chorus: And drill, ye tarriers, drill!
Drill, ye tarriers, drill!
And it's work all day for the sugar in your tea,
Down beyond the railway!
So drill ye tarriers drill, And blast and fire.

**Our new foreman name it was John McCann
And say by God, he was a blame mean man.
Last week a premature blast went off
And a mile in the air went big Jim Goff.**

Next time the payday came around
Jim Goff a dollar short was found!
'What for?' he asked,
and he got this reply 'You were docked for the
time you were up in the sky.'

*Thomas Casey (words) and later Charles Connolly
(music).*

Harvest Song

The apples shine brightly and swing in the breeze,
The corn in the meadow stands tall,
The bramble has covered the hedge with ease,
The harvest delights us all.

The insect that flies for the swallow in flight,
The cone in the forest that falls,
The mushroom that nestles away from the light,
The harvest delights us all.

The trout in the river with silvery gleam,
Vaults high in the waterfall,
The pollen of flowers enfolds the bee,
The harvest delights us all.

The wholesome prize of allotment and field,
The produce will ripen and store,
To nurture and cherish throughout the year,
The harvest delights us all.

Oh, dear, what can the matter be

Oh, dear, what can the matter be
Three old ladies locked in the lavatory,
They were there from Monday to Saturday
Nobody knew they were there.

Waiting at the Church

There was I, waiting at the church,
Waiting at the church,
Waiting at the church;
When I found he'd left me in the lurch,
Lor, how it did upset me!
All at once, he sent me round a note
Here's the very note,
This is what he wrote:
"Can't get away to marry you today,
My wife, won't let me!"

My thanks to Henry E Prther and Fred W Leigh for the happy
times when I heard this song.

Riding down from Bangor

Riding down from Bangor on the eastern train,
After weeks of hunting in the woods of Maine,
Quite extensive whiskers, beard. moustache as well,
Sat a student fellow, tall and slim and swell,
Empty seat behind him, no-one at his side,
Into quiet village eastern train did glide,
Enter aged couple; take the hindmost seat,
Enter village maiden, beautiful petite.

Blushingly she faltered,
"Is this seat engaged?"
See the aged couple properly enraged.
Student quite ecstatic, sees her ticket "Through"
Thinks of the long tunnel
Thinks what he might do.

Pleasantly they chatted; how the cinders fly,
Till the student fellow gets one in his eye,
Maiden sympathetic turns herself about,
"May I, if you please, sir, try to get it out?"

Then the student fellow feels a gentle touch,
Hears a gentle murmur "Does it hurt you much?"
Whiz Slap Bang . into tunnel quite,
Into glorious darkness, black as Egypt's night.

Out into the daylight glides that eastern train,
Student's hair is ruffled just the merest grain,
Maiden seen all blushes when then and there
appeared
A tiny little ear-ring in that horrid student's beard.

A very funny old bird is the pelican
His beak can hold more than his bellican....

El Paradiso

Lettucepray

Our Nirvana
Who art at Screwfix
Hallowed De Walt by name.
Thy catalogues come
Thy drills be spun, with mirth,
As it is on page seven.
Give us this day our safety vests,
And supply us our lens glasses
As we survive those who smash glass around us.
And lead us not into temptation
And deliver us from Homebase.
For thine is the pantheon,
The power tools and the Allen keys,
For fellers more clever than
car-men.

Beaksatdawn

The cygnets fight for river space
With dive bomb jump and flip.
The vicar said he thinks it is
Sibling swan-up-man-ship.

Filmstarbilge

I think that I will never see
A poem lovelier than me.
And me whose sultry south is dressed
Up to my svelte girth's glowing breasts;
For me who thinks I'm God all day
As fits my steamy charms I pray;
And see me in my underwear
A nest of Cheetos in my care;
See how my bosom's pert and new.
(Do I showcase a low IQ?)
Poems are made by ghouls like thee,
But only wads of cash made me.

L'Hitlerature

'Mein Kampf' by Hitler the know-all
Was a book at which nobody laughed
His brother a minor he dug coal
And his book had title 'Mein Schaft'

Tearlingporkies

What a wonderful od'ur the pig are---
When he grunt he speak almost;
Where he live, his stay…. almost.
He ain't got no wings hardly;
He dont get no mail hardly either.
When he sing, he sing 'bout what he ain't
pot or roast. (Yet)

Castle Leaver

I must go down for the cheese again,
and the slice of ham that I fry,
And all I ask, is a scribbled list
and a car to carry me by,
And the traders call and the old town hall
and the old bells ringing,
And the video man and the butcher's van
and hear the clubbers swinging.

I must go down for the cheese again,
for a rag on the shelf that lies,
For a birdseed ball, from a market stall
that sold those old mince pies;
And at Brampton halt, the rail's at fault
and the old train's vanished,
And I hurried on while the sun shone,
cause the old girl's famished.

I must go down for the cheese again,
to the assistant's weary life,
With a working grudge, and a 'Ta shug,'
from a face like netted tripe;
And the tills ring and the tannoys sing
and the milk's all from clover
And time's flew, for the tea's due,
now the short day's over.

Messagent

All were given a green onion surprise
At a fair-like summer treat.
Said the allotment holders 'We'll organise
So come and take a leek.'

Earacheinglytrue

A baby she or he learns to walk and talk
And parents a lot of annoyance will
put up.
But no sooner done
And the battle is won
She'll/He'll be expected to sit down
and shut up.

Uppancecomale

With his new phone the toff called De Vere,
Riled his friends at the pub it was clear,
Later it fell to the floor,
And as he went through the gent's door
They left, with the phone in his beer.

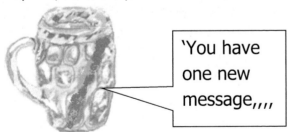

'You have one new message,,,,,

The TV cooking competition 'The Jagged Wok' is entered
by a talented council house lad, from Doncaster.

Grabbawoky

'Twas grilli'g, and the spicy toast
Did fire and tremble and degrade:
All flimsy were the hollow globes,
And the toast racks displayed.

'Beware the Jagged Wok my son!
The cloves that bite, the freaks that watch!
Beware the custard bird, and shun
The glutinous butter-scotch!.

' He took his forthright fork in hand:
Long time the toothsome roe he sought
Ingested he the hung mung bean.
And good lambs fry he bought.

And, there in stylish wrought there stood,
His Asda wok upon the flame
(Came with a lid, as usually would)
He filled it up with game.

Swan too? Gone! Flew! And stew and brew
This portion made was not a snack!
And it is said, he used his head
His own triumphing knack.

And he did gain the Jagged Wok.
Thumbs up! 'Stay calm, Oh steamish boy
Oh fabulous day,' ' O'er moon! Hooray!'
He chuckled in his joy.

Twas brilliant, and the bubbly toasts
Did fire the vict'ry on parade,
All kingsy were the pheromones,
And the home rats outplayed.

Afrimonkham

The baboon has a face like a smudge on a wall,
He dines on leaves which are gathered or fall,
His 'fleece' has grease and harbours fleas,
And at night they'll sleep on the cliffs or in trees.

His calling card is a reeking house
Look he's cowering now at the call of his spouse,,
"Where's y'at," she cries, if he's scared, he'll moon,
But best not like a lout, pick a fight with him soon.

Now if a large male wants to come here and stay,
Trouble can happen I'll keep out of his way,
But if a baboon orphan whimper'ng arrives,
I'll shelter him kindly and feed him pork pies.

Dentyourego

Old Casper crawled on the cinema floor
The attendant alerted was soon through the door.
Can I help you?' he asked and Cas said,
'About a minute ago my gum I spat out'
The attendant, kindly offered Cas some gum,
Cas now looked on a little bit dumb
He crawled to a seat and sat for a minute,
'You don't understand'
That gum had my teeth in it!

Reasus-negatrive

We are all aware
it doesn't take genius
To observe that a man
Has a brain and a penis
But God's thinking 'good'
With his humorous design
By not giving enough blood
To run both at the same time.

Shook-up Shakespeare

Let me not to marriage of two dykes
admit impoverishments.
Life is not life
If sep'rate when the high vacation finds,
Nor blends with the ground coffee to aid strife,
Not white! It is for ever fixed dark,
To look on software and be never shaken.
And in the start of every camping lark,
Which trips alone in woe would not be taken.
Likes not Thai food?
Though noisy chops and steak,
Within their fav'rite modern rest'raunts soon:
Life alters not with her long shifts and breaks,
But bears it out for both until the hols of June.
If they be in Glasgow, in studio improved
They always sit, where no bear ever moved.

The following poem is based on the true incident of a power cut at a _west_ end theatre where, performing in the 'Black and White Minstrel Show' were

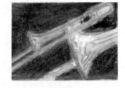

comedians Leslie Crowther and George Chisholm.

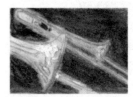

Realising what had happened by hearing the music equipment slow and then fail along with the lights, they grabbed torches and George Chisholm his trombone and ran to the stage, where they entertained the audience until the lights came back on.

Darkumer

A comedy duo,
From what they had heard
Grabbed torches in a power cut
To the stage they were spurred.

They lit each others faces,
And with jokes and trombone,
Entertaining the audience
Who might have gone home.

When the power came back on,
Not heard were stock laughs.
As the duo were revealed
In just their jock-straps.

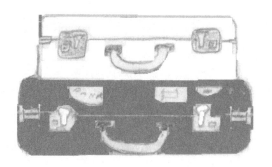

Baggin Court

Once more unto the beach,
dear friends, once more;
And make up the sarnies from our English bread!
At work there's nothing so becomes us all
As modest humour and keen loyalty:

But when the end of term sounds in our ears,
Then imitate the action of the sprinter;
Stiffen the luggage, summon up the passport,
Disguise fair freckled skin with mild flavoured lotion.
Then lend the wallet hearty wads of travellers
cheques;
Let it bulge through the lining of the suitcase Like
the pocket parked apple;

Let unbridled joy o'erwhelm the senses
As wonderfully as do the mem'ries
Of years gone by when beaches were assailed,
Swill'd by th' defiled and waste full ocean
Now set the sat. nav. and service the engine whine,

Hold hard the handles and pile the bulging cases to
their full height!

On, on you merry travellers!
Whose time has come for exit from employment;
You employees, that like so many others,
Have in these parts s'milar exits sought
And packed their bags for imminent departure.

Prepare to follow your neighbours,
who at the barbecue you saw,
Those whom you called friends
and did invite you,
Drink coffee now,
Then join the airline flood,
And gridlock the M4.

And you good children,
Whose inflatables were made in Taiwan,
Show us here
The texture of your ice cream,
let us swear that they are worth their licking;
which I doubt not;

For there is none of you so stayed and blind
That hath not seen the sunshine in the skies.
I see you jump like greyhounds with the ticks,
Straining upon the start.

The hols are here: Follow your parents;
and upon their commands
Cry "Go for Harrich, Ireland or Salerno!"

Kingtututut (Part 1)

We're in Egypt I'm Sandy Tomb
With professor Denial
We're in the valley of the Queen's
We've been here quite a while.

Oh t'was in Baghdad
When my mother met my dad
Singing Nelly put your belly next to mine.

We were told that we would be here
For a week or two at most
But after six years I think I'd miss
Our Sunday camel roast.

We've got some men from Akbar
In the sun yes it's a life
They've come up from the Casbah
Where Prof he found his wife.

But then Assof Ben Tin Ally
Our foreman came from Glynde
'A chaps relieved 'iself in't valley
'e saw do-er way int'er grind"

Searching for some papyrus
The prof asked in whispered talk
Have you got the dead sea Scrolls?
No it's just the way I walk.

We dug our way down to a door
Which looked both thin and dried
A plastic trumpet near a sign
'Said 'Toot and calm in-side.'

The prof he rushed all serene
And peered right through a crack
He screeched and said that he had seen
A green eye looking back

The door pulled open and inside
We heard something like a cough
A voice said **'No, not again**
The alarm will now go off!

Behind the door were things in heaps
Gold relics and ladies' garters
Then someone found a receipt
It had all come from Argos

0020202

A computer shoplifter Jeff Camlets
Went to the Doctor, depressed, in Tower Hamlets
The Doc had a hard drive,
To see this work-skive,
So she told him to keep taking the tablets.

Woodstop

Whose woods are these I think I know.
His locker's in the room below;
These clubs should not be sitting here
But whose they are I do not know.

The club attendant's coming near
And he must think it rather queer
That I look on the table's hoard
Whilst I am tense and waiting here.

He gives his wiry head a shake
To ask (as if!) there's some I'd take
And would my skin begin to creep
To think there's any move I'd make!

The woods are shiny, arched, not cheap,
But on their owner I'll not cheat,
For I'll be honest and be brief
I'm just a poem pinching thief.

Gaylord

(A Knight and a Reeve meet on a road near the
King's castle.)
'Good Sir Knight, how faireth our aged King? Are
we to be blessed with an heir?' '
Alas Reeve, he is still intent upon bedding local
knaves.'
Then abandon hope as his life enters its final
chapter?'
'Aye, though I dare say..... it will run to a good
few more pages.'

Footballer's Wife

Shall I compare thee to a weathered rake?
Thou art less useful and more delicate:
New gowns do cause the normal press affray,
And lacking is your common sense to date:
Sometimes too high the height of cashpile flies,
And oft is our fooled compr'hension dimmed:
And every change of hair your spouse decides,
Compares to rounded haystack pile now strimmed;
But thy eternal blandness shall not fade,
Nor lose the measure of those breasts you bought,
Nor shall dull Brit take thy image to their aid,
When in nocturnal times to bed they hoard;
So long as men shall thieve, we wish to see,
Less large excess, and greed give life to thee.

Elizoneliners

The Duchess disliked the Royal dogs,
To shoot the corgis best pleases,
On hearing this Queen Elizabeth said,
"They're better behaved than she is.'

The trials of Fashion Slave Kate

Thrice the thin-fed Cath hath stewed,
Spies her lumps, her edge big-lined?
Shaplier thighs in time must find,
Frowned about the cord run grow;
Thin the choisest bent rails throw,
Moan, chat on the gold phone,
Gaze at tights size thirty one?
Sheltered heaven, creeping bot,
Toil now cursed in the balmed plot.

Stunner struggle, toil at stubble;
Lither yearn, and suction double.

Rip the carton, foil and bake;
Dye to suit, by blow of smog,
Cull of plait and pong of dog.

Chavver's talk, at fine perms spring,
Frizzards edge while jowlets swing,
For the calm of direful trouble,
Like gel-Goth's buoyant double.

Stunner struggle, toil at stubble;

Lither yearn, and suction double.
Rail of rags by youth in sulk;
Riches! Come see more-and gulp
Of the severe short pleat scarf;
Boots on leg long rigg'd f'the park;
Slither to a teeming queue;
Pour on coat, it slips on you,
Silver'd are the jewels she clips;
Pose and lark, if ra-ra fits?

Order of girth strangled cape
Quick delivered by a cab,-
Make accrual quick and grab:
And tear to a chider's floor-run
For the indulgencies of lost caution.

Stunner struggle, toil at stubble;
Lither yearn, and suction double.

Fools we hope you understood,
Fashion's charm is skin-deep crud.

Buttwattittpores

The rain it raineth every day
Upon the just and unjust caller,
But mainly on the just, because
The unjust has the just's fedora.
(With apologies to Charles Bowem)
ageing poetry lovers meet

He said – She said

He – I drink in your pink chin.
She thinks - Both of them?

She – You fill up my séances
He thinks – It was love at first fright.

He – A face that launched a thousand ships. She
thinks – More like a place that scoffed thousand
chips.

She – You are a fine figure of a man, my Lochinvar.
He thinks – A pity it's a figure 8.

He – You walk in beauty like the night.
She thinks – But I ought to lose the cape and fangs.

She – Fly me to the moon.
He thinks – Where else would I take an alien?

He – I'll watch 'Young Frankenstein' again.
She thinks – I had noticed that bolt in your neck.

Gobitall

The doctor told me 'eat more fruit '
(There's a good shop in the village)
And take all your medication.'
(Thinks 'That says it all!')
A life of grape and pillage.

The Iphone Expose

The Lord is my iPhone;
I shall dark font.

He maketh me to scroll down in streamed
pixels
He tweeteth me beside the sync portal.

He diverteth my call: He selphieth me
In the paths of frequencies for his games'
sake.

Yea, though I swipe through the
warehouse of the carphone of
death,
I will fear no iPod: for iCloud art
with me;
Thy blog and thy app they comfort me.

Thou installest a cable before me
in the presence of my accessories

Thou anointest my Tech with foil:
My hub runneth over.

Surely twooshness and cookies shall follow
me
all the days of my swipe:
And I will text in the house of O2
for ever.

Godotwitless

Because I could the bus not stop
(O death think on for me)
In town I toured
Ikea shop where
God bought eternity?

Awaywithwords

Two more row, and too follow and to swallow.
Neeped this pretty plaice from gravy say
To the vast grillable of afforded thyme.
And haul of chef's days have blighted drools
(The wait drew Trusty Beth.)
Out, shout leek scandal.
Th'wife's butter forking yellow, on floor greyer.
Then chucks and rests her flour upon the sage
And then is curd no more. Bit in a stale
Roll by itinerants, full for browned off brew'y -
Signal; Defying huffing.

Vestedinterest

To take his cash with him planned Miser Mc Lockets
He searched but he found no shroud had pockets
(The ideas of rich folk! We'll call them 'fruit cases')
He went out and purchased two asbestos suit cases

We advise that you should reduce your intake of imitation fruit fizzy concoctions if you wish to reduce your carbonated footprint.

Risqué Business

Dawncame

The nurse asked my pal Dixie
How he had broken his leg
'Twenty years ago it was nearly
When I worked on a farm near Cliffedge

One hot summers day in the hay barn
I was working when Maisy walked in
She was eighteen and really good looking
And her face had an odd sort of grin

She said there was no one else on the farm
And was there anything I wanted to do
Well I said 'No thanks' but she asked me again
She said '' Something happy I could do with you.'

And this morning high up by the chimney
Like a horse kicked me with its 'oof
I twigged and knew what she was after
And that's when I fell off the roof.

Date a Dictionary

Picture it for yourself
there I was sitting
In an up market Lesbian restaurant,
Sorry Lebanese restaurant
Opposite Hedda Précis,
A stunning Lexicographer
Currently re-writing the OED no less.

I was having a little dalliance,
i.e. having a night away from
my long-time partner Theandre.
It was one of those phrases
you go through when we'd reached a period,
where I felt the need to
dash off and instigate another introduction.
The contents of my life having become a little type
cast.

Hedda had a degree
(Though she claimed she'd got it,
by plagiarising her
fathers finals paper answers
– a blatant case of parent thesis
– if ever I heard one.)

Hedda was bright alright
But that wasn't what I'd Met her for!
My eyes were drawn
to her Aglobe pepetua split infinitives
that I wished to fontle.
At this point Subjunctivitis
was franklin an ocular possibility.

Then Hedda sneezed,
(she'd obviously caught an inflection),
And this may have been a signal,
(the subtext to all this was probably
what she had been doing
with her mobile phone under the table)
For in walked my lady

Yeah Thea saw us!
And abbreviated our relationship
before a crossword had been said.
'What kind of an idiom do you take me for',
Bawled Thea. (Scene deleted)
Well that put a full stop to it all.
I was out in the Britannic bold
Definitely comic, sans the humour
And the whale thing makes me [sic]

The Dunnock

Researched and logged and put on air
The bird the dunnock defies compare.
With parents three or four or five
Their avian genes to keep alive.

So it's red-hot coupling – whey hey hey
Up to one hundred times a day.
She poses ready and then he starts
He 'pecks' her rear-end proffered parts

Reducing the load left by his rival
Increasing his progeny's survival.
This occurs in many a coupling
Perhaps described as joyous ruttling.

Then in a flash that's almost brutal
(Blink and you'll miss it)
He's in and out and in less than a second
and they're off.
(No time even for a rhyme)

Gardengorp

A naked old lady passed two men reclining,
Gone quickly she left them ruefully smiling
One said, ' Did you see what she wore?'
The other 'No, but there's one thing I'm sure'
Whatever it was needed ironing.'

Brainifried

She works in the chip shop
It's apt 'cause she's hot.
'Can I help you?' she asks
(I think 'not a lot!')

'Chicken and chips please'
She asks 'Breast or leg?"
My mind's in a frenzy
But heavy as lead
In an echoy cave
I hear my voice
Light years away..... say
'I don't know,
(Fizzing in hand – dynamite)
'What are your breasts like?'
Aaaaaaahhhhhhh

(Swift exit not followed by a bear
But just as fast)

Sexybeasts

A Zombie's no good as a bonker
'Cause his sex anatomics are dead
And though Frankenstein's frame is a stonker
But his part might be too small in bed.

With Godzilla you'll need a physician
If you ever ask him to 'give head,'
And the Mummy's long time for coition
Will probably make you see red

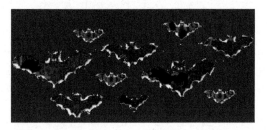

So the vampire's the sexiest monster
Though a relationship's bound to be strained
But you may say 'By heck he's a pain in the neck'
And you may feel a little bit drained.

Pataquery

Lin thought it best
to ask her pa
As spare cash she had
by working hard.
She thought that
she could now afford
a boyfriend or a car.
Her dad didn't like
to burst her bubble
He said –
(His mouth ringed with stubble)
'Your worries they will double,
If it's got tyres or tentacles
It'll give you trouble.'

Weightabit

Why are married women, on average, heavier than
single women?
A single woman comes home, goes to the fridge and
goes to bed.
.A married woman comes home, looks in the bed and
goes to the fridge.

Hadvice

His chances of sex were their darkest
So Viagra was prescribed by Doc. Harkness.
Then his friend asked 'Now Bill
What's it like on that pill?'
'Well the first seven days were the hardest.'

Disinbragate

At a wedding a maid from Loire
Was pinched by her low strapless bra
She loosened one wire
Her dress fell entire
And her face went the hue of foie gras.

Wellsorted

On a hospital ward Mary Hepper
Had symptoms that wouldn't get better
She found that each sneeze
A fulfilment bequeathed
And the remedy's simple - it's pepper.

Chinese Emperor Concubines

After 5000 girls were collected
Whittled down, very few were selected.

By height, weight and voice
They made their choice

By one means or another
All aspects to cover.

From the few who were left
After they had all slept

A night with the Emperor's mother.
(Presumably to check for snoring?)

1950s Spain

In bikinis two mums on the beach
Were quizzed at length by two police.
As the costumes preferred
were all of one piece.
One mum smiled and gave an amused cough.
'Which is the piece you'd like me to take off?'

The Theatrical Impresario who gets a mauling in the press.

Interred

'The smallest room is where I sit,
A gesture not meant kindly.
In front of me your scissored crit,
Will shortly be behind me.'

Life Savour

A splash of colour
In my blurred vision.
Hoisted above the wet deck,
Sitting serene,
seventeen and unflustered.
Ever watchful for unsurfaced swimmers.
Long limbed, legs akimbo,
Scarlet shirt and short-shorts.
Our loose limbed lookout,
We all depend on you.

Stereo-trypes

This writer here you'll say he lied
(And after he was vilified)
For telling of a sad event
But to depress was never meant.
He spread the word to all he knew
A story he averred was true
(A sea tale that's in no way dull,)
but probably apocryphal.

The ship it sailed well out of view
Replete with tourists, stores and crew,
But tragedy was yet in store
Ineptitude the Captains flaw,
The mighty vessel struck a reef
And quickly was soon underneath
the waves, and leaving mournful cries
Of those who had, with luck, survived.

They landed on th'uncharted isle
A place that would the mind beguile,
A land perhaps of recent birth
You'll find it not on Google earth.
And gathered there upon the sand
A very cosmop'litan band
Of people who that we could say
Were glad to be alive that day.

There were Two Italian men and one woman,
Two Greek men and one woman,
Two French men and one woman,

Two German men and one woman,
Two English men and one woman.

The Italians were a touch extreme,
In manner not at all serene,
The males, Benito and Caesar
Began a heated sharp fracas
They really had a lot to gain
O'er who should bed the fair Helene
And she was filled with fear and dread
When Caesar shot Benito dead.

And in the sun the handsome Greeks
Had partied on, all laughs and shrieks,
Cavorting wildly in the sea
(It would have made some cheap TV)
The men had then both disappeared
The woman searched but as she feared,
(You could have felled her with a feather)
She found them bedded well together.

The French were in a blissful state,
Their joie de vivre I can relate
Was fulsome rounded and I found
They made a most arousing sound
For they, Oh Yes, were making hay,
And all at once I have to say
A carry on, a la-di-da
A carefree blissful ménage a trois.

The Germans they were organised
(No 'sturm und drang'! You'd be surprised,)
The Frau she had no lasting doubts
She didn't want two sour Krauts,
For bedroom time filled with delight
She'd framed and mounted in plain sight,
A schedule which we all could tell
Was typed and printed on excel.
(By contrast however.....)

The English folk were looking glum
As hush! Keep schtum! Was rule of thumb,
And they were looking tense and stressed
As if some crime had been confessed.
The silence had an air of dread
For no word had as yet been said,
And then the answer was produced
No one had been introduced.

Mmmm He's hot!

'But me speak first. NO WAY!'

Adapted from an article in the Welsh Friendsheep Ewespaper

Billionaire Immorald Chump
forcibly purchased
An area of coastline near Borth,
Including all the larger sand hills,
(Used for stamina building by Olympic trainers)
And in incandeescent haste
had them fenced them off
with barbed wire.
Much to the fierce opposition of the local population.
Privately it is believed,
through ear witness reports of fires
and strange chantings,
that the land has been given over
to certain groups who revere satanic worship. Signs
attached to the wire meant to deter athletes
and day walkers
say the site has been declared an SSSI though the
rather overblown
graffiti may be more accurate :
Site of sodomite saturnalian insidiousness.
That's the situation,   I can comment no further
Except to remark that in Borth it would seem
the devil has all the best dunes.

Well Beggarme

Barbra Less wed Paul and Les
Against our British law
And we all know
That this will show
The needs of Less is more.

Marriage – a man's view

A wife is there to help a man
Through all the troubles
He wouldn't have had
If he hadn't got married.

Whosecountin

'I'm tired,' said the pretty young Swede,
'That's twice I've not slept until three.'
The other replied
'No wonder you're tired.'
'For it's twice that is all that I need.

Bangersandashed

He came down quite undressed,
Except a crimson garter.
'This national sausage day', he stressed
I've obeyed the Royal Charter.'

His wife feigned no surprise,
In quick-thinking she was smarter
She said, 'The charter's text revised
Was for the chipolata.'

LimerIQck

The lovers of limericks are no seers,
In hearing lewd things they've no fears.
And when comes the times,
They are hearing rude rhymes,
Why they all turn and prick up their ears.

It's All Out There

John Major on the cover
When his book it hit the shelves
As Edwina his lover
Gerald Scarf cartooned their selves.
She in bed, eyes scheming, topless.
Grey Major climbs the bed
Her hand plays with his firmness.
Was 'Back to Basics' bred?

Thetalldoit

The sexual urge of the camel
Is greater than anyone thinks.
After several months in the desert,
It attempted a rape on the Sphinx.
Now, the intimate parts of that lady
Are sunk 'neath the sands of the Nile.
Hence the lump on the back of the camel
And the Sphinx's inscrutable smile.

Artillery camp, Cairo, 1940.

Econotruthmy

A man was asking his good wife
After fifty three years they'd been wed,
Had she been unfaithful in their married life
And she recalled three times she said.

The first time was when you needed a loan,
To the new business you were inclined.
The bank manager swore at you over the phone
Well I did what made sure that he signed.

And then in your forties that scare with your heart
And the best surgeon was ace Dr. Strauss.
He wanted help but hadn't time to take part
Well I persuaded him here in this house.

The last time was at the golf club
You wanted to be 'top dog of the fort'
You got elected because I made sure
You weren't fifty seven votes short......

Arsolegobshite

The first edition of 'Huckleberry Finn' had to be
pulped as someone illustrating the book, no doubt
to get back at Mark Twain for repeatedly rejecting
the illustrations as being 'not good enough',
included a male Pisa tower into the design.

Taxidermerick

His two monkeys died and George Sands
Went down to stuff them in Cannes
His opinion was sounded
Did he want them both mounted?
He said, 'No thanks – just shaking hands.'

Kimonot

In Japan, in the nineteenth century, woodblock
printed pornography called 'shunga' showing
every imaginable situation, always involved the
participants wearing clothes mainly because nudity
was so common in society. Copies of this book
were sometimes given as wedding presents.

Tangoed

Mark lusted the squire's lass and sought her
And they had done what they really didn't oughter
His Lordship got plarstered
And said 'Mark, you barstard -
You're not going to marry my daughter.'

Uchoose

'Tonight you can have super sex'
She ignored his brewer's droop
'Thanks' he said in a needless text '
I'll just have the soup.'

Isigonisitus

Luxury and my old mini
Were opposites of logics
Not much cost spread thinly
But painful on the coccyx

Best not hit a rail or kerb
For your knees would crack and lock
A jolt that really was absurd
A force twelve seismic shock.

With tall Tom in the back seat
Joking on the whole uncouth,
I drove over something hard
And Tom's head hit the roof.

The fan belt did sometimes break
You'd never one to hand though
So you used your girlfriend's tights
If she'd not gone 'commando'

An engine change on garage floor
Was full festooned detritus
And I think that was the night
That I got gasketitus.

Swedish campers helped us when
The battery had 'lost charge;
They pushed, the engine then kicked in
They shouted 'Flying – start'

One night the smell of burning
To the boot I was not slow
Inside I was gobsmacked to see
A miniature fireworks show.

Amphibirsveup

To the hop, came the frogs, of Hong Kong
They had also invited James Pond
They were toad it was okee
To dance the Hoakey Croaky
And drink wine a tad Polish and strong

Pompeiilian

(Tune – The Red Flag)
O Priapus - Please mind that bus
It's in your panorama
O Priapus or you'll be such
As flat as ham from Palma.
And stroking you I'm calmer
Your rear view it is a charmer.
It can't be true! O what a view!
Just like a pencil sharp'ner

119

Catholichouse

In the bedroom wardrobe I hide
I watched the priest and mum,
Then I heard Dad's car arrive
The priest moved at a run.

Next I knew he's in with me
He's no idea (a voice inside me' said.)
So I said, 'Isn't It's dark in here,?'
He jumped and banged his head.

My blackmail got me forty quid
But mum soon got to know
She screamed **'Think what you did!'**
To confession I must go.

Inside sitting down I said,
'Isn't it dark in here?'
His shout it knocked my head,
'Now don't start that again!'

Chop chop

The male adult'rers in hell
what a scene!
Smug throngs
- tossed their manlibits,
how obscene,
Then Old Nick with a smile
Led them to a small aisle
Which lead to small guillotine.

Gympumpndnotbeprim

BUILD YOUR NEW BODY

Inspirational stuff, the ultimate sign?
I'll pump the iron, I'll not decline.
(Later)
On second thoughts I'll not to waste their time.
But I'd build a body - It just wouldn't be mine.

Fangs for the Memory

If Dracula's trailing your wife
There's bound to be a disturbance,
And beware if he offers eternal life
He's <u>not</u> trying to sell you insurance.

Sparkey

It looked like fireman Bob
Would be good at his job,
His strength to fight fires his heart promised.
And things went as they do
But none of them knew,
That his hobby was that of an arsonist.

The more you weigh,
The harder you are to kidnap.

SO STAY SAFE
EAT CAKE.

And celebrate Rover's birthday.

Miss Cellany

Hellofaplace

In hell Satan greeted newly damned,
He stated the agonies his henchmen use
That if he heard would him _{amuse}
He then went through some thousand rules
Including his sadistic views
(For heaven's sake
Let's not say of him ill
He'd only eternity to fill)

And by taking FAQs
And by giving them infernal news
And by adding striking wit
He'd not allowed anyone a seat
For what must have felt a week.
His rants their hope to disabuse
He really thought he could not lose
(He'd worn out several autocues)
And then he mentioned
Made it clear
That no there were no loos
or toilets here
'Of course' was heard
With stuttered grief
Damnation is without relief.

Then someone sneered and asked
If in his career
He had met with being
Far or near
Had caused some cold dampening
of his skin,
Or scared the willies out of him?

Smoke poured out of Satan's face
and many another orifice
Some of them unmentionable
Unless you're seeking some relief
In situation medical
Let's just say we'd better know
If he'd then at once turned round
(And then we'd also hear the sound
Of buttocks vibrating long and loud
And later we might also tell
That there was a noxious smell
Emitted with demonic art
A fuming wreaking fanfare...

**'WAS THAT YOU MIKE VAN DAM?
LISTEN WELL AND FEAR MY WRATH
I AM AFRAID OF NOUGHT
THAT YOU COULD VISUALIES WITHIN THAT
PEANUT MINISCULE OF THOUGHT
THAT YOU CALL A MIND
THAT MOST OTHERS BUT SOMETIMES FEWER
REFER TO AS YOUR CLOGGED MANURE.'**

And at that moment Mike was seen
SLAMMED RIGHT THROUGH THE FLOOR
And loud was heard his heartrending scream.
Said Satan now in full ranted strop,
Repeating all we've heard before
And at that moaning so profound,
from a million voices now occurred -
which covered Old Nick's mumbling sound.
So no one the end of sentence heard
That fear crept out listlessly and ran......

'Except the occasional White Van Man.'

Vatertherapy

It happened on a Polynesian isle,
No high blown story to beguile,
The strong Wakiki lived within his tribe
And he had a bad luck we can describe
(Though scamp he was, he hadn't sinned)
His suffered with the most appalling wind.
Which all agreed was way beyond the limit
When you were caught and held within it.

His friends then found a bottle on the shore
They didn't know the liquid that it bore
It had a pungent, aromatic smell
And it looked green as far as they could tell.
It seemed to offer hope of cure
If it could pass o'er Wakiki's jaw
So they held him down and dosed him up
Poured down his throat cup after cup.

Imagine though (it made them curse)
It only made the smell get worse!
So to the village elder made their way
And asked him all at once if he could say.
What was the cure for this affliction
And he replied in clearest diction.
'You lads have tried to mend this fault,
I'm pleased though that you've called a halt

We'd all be better off if it was found
To cure Wakiki's pong and steamship sound.
I'll not berate you any longer
You see...
Absinthe makes the fart grow stronger.

126

Goodvibrater

Liking her more as she grows older
The archaeologist loves his wife,
Never known to give the cold-shoulder
She is the carnal bed rock of his life.

The Yearnings of J. L. Bird

I am described by all my friends
As an exemplary man.
I work for naught for many hours
And give help when I can.

I do not smoke and seldom drink
Or mess around with women,
And all of this is going to change
When I get out of prison.

Vacant

It's just like I've always said,
His bed he will not leave
And so I said get out of bed
And then he says to me
(Chorus)
On work I am not crazy
That is no joke or jape
So you think I am lazy
MY eyesight has gone hazy
Just peel me another grape.

Hoppimissed

The firm knew no shirker
Was draughtsman R. Moulders
A very balanced worker
He'd a chip on both shoulders.

Whoever he'd talk to
Something would always offend,
With eye threat he'd spike you
A clear message he'd send.

His mind like a slow cooker
A thousand mile trough,
Brewed up his grudges
That had left him hacked off.

So if seen approaching
To avoid most were lead
And if with his wife
Well, the panic spread.

He retired - had some good years
Though some irony was known,
For he spent his last years
In 'The Grouse Nursing Home.'

1717

The bible of John Basket's case
Produced a cartload of mistakes
The word 'Vineyard' came out like 'Linacre'
As in 'The parable of the 'vinegar'

128

This is based on my time looking after a volunteer allotment,

Lum Bard

Hello backache my old friend
I've come to know you as I bend,
Above the soil the Jenny was creeping
And it left its seeds that I was treating
And the feeling that was planted in my spine,
While I recline,
Became the pound of backache.

And at the plot I worked alone,
Finding glass and bits of bone
With no shelter from the cold and damp,
I made the soil into a three foot clamp
When my fingers were stamped by the sting,
of a nettle's leaf,
I grit my teeth
And that was with the backache.

And in the new raised bed I saw
Ten thousand dock plants maybe more
The bed I saw myself it was leaking,
And the answer that I was seeking,
And the restfulness that muscles never got
I'd lost the plot
Which meant a lot of backache

Fools said I, I did not know
Why comfrey like a true weed grows.
For it causes pain that is profound,
My joints were making a creaking sound,
When the comfrey needed strimming with a knife,
We'll get a life,
Added to the backache.

And Robert wrestled with a spade
Near the heap that he had made,
And Dean he shouted out a loud warning
That the thunder clouds they were forming, And as
Lisa saw the fall of the
Water on the tunnel door we all withdraw,
To contemplate the backache.

Austenalia

It is a truth, triggered by morality,
that a married lady, biting the bullet of waning self
respect, due to her husband's denied affairs with
nubile blondes, must be in need of
an AK 47.

Anne a primary school teacher is on an arranged date with Mac an uncouth, loud-mouthed, unintelligent, scaffold erector who hasn't showered. Sally, Anne's friend whose idea this was, said that she'd been told Mac was 'well endowed' and that he drives a sports car. The latter, as Anne knows to her cost is definitely true - he seriously scared her, on their trip to the restaurant and he is now making obscene comments while eating his pork leg noisily.

(The singer needs to have a burly chassis)

Umekmepuke

The minute you hawked up a joint,
I could see you were a man of expunction,
A real sick gender,
Flood puking, so reviled.
Nay you wouldn't be likely to know what's going
on in my mind!
So maybe you'll now get the point,
I don't drop my chalk for ev'ry man I see
HEY rig mender,
Wend a little while I flee.

Wouldn't I like to have fun? Fun? RUN!
(Holds nose)
If you'd take a few baths! BATHS!
Your tattoo is a - bad sign
Oh you say that you've – done time!

You idiot you don't get the point,
I can see your fire is now in extinction,
A real dim ember!

(Mac leaves table to pick up a dropped fork revealing his builder's bum.)
Butt crooked, so behind.
Nay you wouldn't be likely to know what's going on in my mind!
You still have not quite got the point,
I would rather date an ape from Mozambique
HEY Pig blender, HEY Stick vendor, HEY Stig minger
END ___ this sick'ning time with me.

Spouscular

A Florida State Trouper
Saw a speeding Land Rover
While returning from duty
So he pulled the guy over.
He told the driver
'It's the end of my tour
So if you can give me a good reason
Why your speed was so high
I'll issue a warning
And charge I'll ignore.'
The driver replied
'My wife, she left me
For a Trouper like you
And I don't miss her
Believe me neither would you.
It's good of you officer
To cut me some slack
You see I took-off thinking
You were bringing her back.

A father is advising his clearly gifted aknoledged 3* Tyre
company son to not be critical of his peers and not to over
eat if he gets stressed.

Iffingitus

If you can keep your bread when all about you
Are chewing theirs and baking hot and new.
If you ban crust yourself will all men shout you?
While fake allowance for their drowning stew.
If soup you hate yet not congratulating
Or seeing fried a trout, don't squeal at pies,
Or remonstrating, allow delay when plating,
And yet don't cook too good, Nor crow or whine.

If you don't baulk at crowds and hide that hurt you,
Nor talk down things, or use the phrase 'as such',
If neither nose nor girl-friends can divert you,
She'll offer ounce for you, but you'll not touch.
And if you cannot deal with slimming limit
And eat fifty neckend's worth of instant bun,
Yours is the girth and everything's gone in it,
And—s'ndwiches more!—you will expand, my son!

Hymenopera

I am pondering whether to write a singing drama
based on the environmental plight of bees and
wasps.
Naturally it will include a wordless buzzing chorus,
many aerial curving melodies with a flower duet or
two. I'll probably hive off the task of writing the
libretto and the finale will be momentous, since that
will be when the fat lady stings.

133

Soundslikerchorus

Oh David you're a funny one
Got a face like a Spanish onion
Got a nose like a squashed banana
And legs like match sticks.

Phonia

Oh give me a phone,
Made in plastic and chrome,
With a qwerty keyboard for my play,
Where my thumbs it's averred,
Will fire up in a blur,
And the time will slip by 'til I'm grey.
I'll drone on the phone,
And be thrilled as a dog with a bone,
and I'll twitter and tweet,
with the folks I'll ne'er meet,
and all of my cash has been blown.

Oh give me an app,
That does not need a strap,
And a tablet that's not made to suck,
And glasses that kind,
That get into your mind,
And providers that'll give me no truck.
I'll email (so chaste)
By employing the old cut and paste,
And when I've paid for broadband,
With an arm and a hand,
I'll adjust the broad band round my waist.

Hard up

(Based on a true on a genuine court case)
A bloke from Stoke
Half-inched some Viagra
In court he was called –
(Police gave him agra,)
His defence it was minimal
'Not a hardened criminal!'
Then the judge Justice Flint-Harsh
Granted him a discharge.

Scotwonders

Is it fair to see a Scotsman
Be he from Edinburgh or Leith,
Digging out a sixpence,
From a dunghill with his teeth?

And all the Gordans can't be gay
Or should we our best wishes send?
And are the Virginias real
Or will that discussion end?

Do you have to come from Fife
The fife and drum to play?
And do the Scottish theatres
Ever stage 'the Scottish Play.'

That's all from me today
My welcome I've abused.
The Scot's say I must 'Go away'
Though that's not the phrase they used.

Note to the prison Dartmoor Prison Governor

It isn't easy, you'll not think strange,
When I try to explain how I feel.
That I need out o'jug
After all that I've dug,

You won't release me.
All you will see is a man locked away,
Dreaming he'll get at the loot
And others will covet it too.

Inevitably it happened, I was sent down
But couldn't stay all my life in this cell,
Looking out of the window,
Wishing I'm in the sun.,

I'd chosen blackmail,
Swanning around coercing.
Everyone knew.
And the 'Old Bill' they knew it too.

**Don't cry for me, Dartmoor Prison
The truth is, I never left you
I tunnelled sideways
A tunnelling novice
I came up in -
the boss'es office!**

Chased

My father went courting
A lass name of Hortin,
From Lancashire quarter
A brass ring he bought her.

He noticed her scent
(It cost more than his rent)
He asked quite banal
Was it 'Eau De Canal.?'

Her mum from the south
Said 'Never put in your mouth
(Even when you're well oiled)
What hasn't been boiled!'

One night on gin tipsy
She ran off wi' gypsy
(D H Lawrence invoked?)
Years later, he joked

She had lips just like petals
(That's bicycle petals.)
And teeth like the stars
(They came out at night.)

Lebanesium

The chief defect of Zaida Zing
Was needing of an uplift thing,
So then she reasoned - in her prime
And booked the operation's time.

Phoenicians of the utmost fame
Were called at once, and called by name
They answered, 'Yes,' (upon their knees)
Their bodies wracked with greed disease,
And she knew what they hoped to gain.

Her parents stood about and said,
'Will Zaida look like camel pet,'
Then she with her gargantuan breaths
Cried, 'Oh my friends that I still see,
My uplift hides a lot of me,
And now I need in stashed Bel Aire
Is randy single millionaire'

More Aptly Chosen Memorial Trees

Fire researcher.	Laburnum
French bridge builder.	L'arch
Ace comedian.	Laurel
Plane speaker	Lilac
Concrete researcher.	Lime
Paint salesman	Magnolia
Vulcanologist.	Mountain Ash
WW II Naval Designer.	Mulberry
Popeye.	Olive

138

Chasedergeld

And did those feet in patient lines,
Wait upon Sainsbury's cash machine:
And was this wholly fanned in wads,
From England's 'gregious banks obsene!

And did the counter dance supine,
File more upon their mounted tills?
And was John Lewis store builded here,
To sting with stark gigantic bills?

Bring me my Rover sprayed like gold;
Bring me the cruiser I desire:
Bring me my beer: in happy'our sold!
Bring me my p'wer-drive on hire!

I will not cease from cost-cut flight,
Nor shall I stay my credit hand:
As they have built a new Poundland,
In England's greed infested land.

Spandiculous

After having a minor tiff with his partner, Pete a mature college student, was walking along a beach in California when he came upon bottle tossing in the waves.

After some effort he managed to remove the cork. Immediately smoke poured out of the bottle and (you've guessed it) a genie appeared.

'At last!' thundered the Genie, sending out a huge shock wave which sent Pete cart wheeling across the sand. He picked himself up and the Genie said, 'Greetings master, you have rendered me a great service; in return I will grant you one wish

'Well I don't fly and I'd like to go on holiday to Hawaii, so could you build me a bridge?' The Genie paused and thought for a few seconds.

'That's quite a large undertaking, master, is there anything else that would do instead?' Now it was Pete's turn to think. 'I'd really like to know why when my lady gets upset she says 'No' when she really means 'Yes.'

The Genie gave a wry smile and putting his arm around shoulder said,

'That bridge? Was that a one lane or two?

Parkmessaging

The Englishman's dog not overwrought
In the park he takes him for a walk.
Sniffing around
Studying the ground
Happiness in mannerly thought

Now I think 'What could be more normal?'
Dogs rarly act in manner formal
The canine's a lurcher
He won't ever 'ertcha'
And the man dresses fairly informal.

He'll usually listen in amused way
If you stop and offer your 'newsday'
(But don't no don't ever
Mention the weather
If you've got an appointment next Tuesday)

(The dog not happier with three tails)
He yearns for curved-hot-fit females
Whose exercise traction
Sliding ski fashion,
While the intelligent dog reads his weemails.

Dogsholmer

I work at Mactavishes
Down Canine Lane
Aye, in the dogs' hame
We have three pregnant poodles
Two of which produced only last night.
Now you might well be askin y'self..
(Mob phone rings)
Scuse me, Yes, hellooo, (listens)
Wonderful. Noo problem.
Sorry, have t'rush
We've a few more mouths t'feed
Just need t, pick up another tin o'Tesco's doggy
pudding for this wonderful breed
I mustnee pause for thought
For you know what we say
At Mactavishes'.......

Every Poodle whelps.

Myistory

After many stressful events
Arguments that became
Punching brawls.
I told my piano teacher
I had got my mum
To leave homebase
Pushed her into it -
She said

142

'I don't want to live
by a butcher's shop'
I said 'I did this to
Keep you out of A & E
Or worse.'
He wouldn't come after her
It was her only chance.
And I'd taken on a debt
The bank needed repaying.'

(Later) We were in a quiet house
in Burslem in 1974
When a noisy family
(Just normal family noise)
Moved in next door.
The mother of this family
Worked in a club in Stoke.
Word got round that she
Was seeing another bloke.

The husband 'smuggled'
a loaded rifle into the house
No one near knew
from where or how.
Had we known
Us hereabout
It could have been
Someone's last shout.

On the night it happened
She came home in a car
He was waiting

With door ajar
He jumped out
James Bond style and
Through an open window -
He poked the gun in
Aimed up and fired.
He aimed to frighten
Which he did
And that's the truth
And maybe damaged hearing
Plus some big holes in the roof.

A lot of shouting
Then broke out.

Through all this I was 'spark out'
The next day when I was about
Asked what had I heard
And in Stoke now I said 'nowt.'

Two policemen came round
Picked him up rough style.
Feet right off the ground
The butcher later
told me and smiled.

He also said
The smile now gone
His eyes irate
The bloke in the car
Was not her bed mate.

The story goes.....

A little old lady is on the phone to the police because in the darkness lit up by a few street lamps, she can see in her garden a large animal that she doesn't recognise.
The policeman thinking the lady is mistaken asks what the animal looks like.
The old lady replies that it is very large, has four legs and a tail at each end.
The policeman still in some disbelief asks 'And could you tell me what is doing in your garden?'
'He's pulling up my cabbages and I'm not going to tell you where he's putting them.'

Wi' 'eart 'n' Sole

The Chic of the Desert
*(Written after watching the rich Arabs and
their racing camels, which they love.)*

The camel pageant's back in town,
And Abdul's beast looks pretty
Botoxed, prepped and blow-waved down,
By the best hands in the city.

But now Abdul looks rather grim
For it's undignified
The use of Botox is a sin
And he's been disqualified.

So what's the moral from the east
The folly is quite gritty
You can't improve the haughty beast
Designed by a committee.

Dipstick Talking

He said ' No I will not.....
threw his mobile on the floor
proceeded to stamp heavily on it
He stopped the mobile started ringing –
(with a dazed expression
perhaps my look he knew)
he lifted up the phone and said 'Oh it's you

Leargnoramus

The Ghoul and the Rusty-bat went to sea
On the usual green-lean goat,
They took some dummies, and twenty two bunnies,
Bagged up with a live browned stoat.
The Ghoul looked up to the bars above,
And sang to a small sitar,
"O lovely Rusty! O Rusty my love,
What a dutiful fruity you are,
You are, You are!
What a yecchiful muffty you are!"

Rusty said to the Ghoul, "O elephant jowl!
How disarmingly effete you sing!
O let us be carried! Too strong we have harried:
But what shall we do for a cling?"
They railed away, for a merman at bay,
To the land where the Wrong-Tree grows
And there in a wood a Jig-earwig stood
With a ring at the end of his toes,
His toes, His toes,
He will cling 'til the end of his woes.

"Dear Jig, can we orange to sell for two florins
Your ring?" Said the Jiggy, "I vill."
So they chucked it away, and were carried next day
To the turnkey who lives near to Rhyl.
They dined off chintz, and splices of mints ,
Which they ate with a discernible croon;
And rand in hand, on a ledge on the Strand,
They pranced like a flight of baboon,
baboon, baboon,
They flounced with the fright of poltrunes.

Elevating Situation

An aged lady Margaret Brown,
At Waldorf suite in New York town
Was descending in the lift alone
The box now slowed, with braking tone
And in walked three unnerving men.
Their looks were grim and threatening then
With seeming spite, to Marg they turned around
And one says, 'Ok Grandma, HIT THE GROUND!'
So down she hastens to comply
But to her aid the men reply
By helping her back to her feet
And courteously (to her relief)
She was assisted out and to a taxi cab
It was unthinkable that anyone they'd stab.

(later) Mag never saw the men again
She looked out often but in vain.
And when she left where she had stayed
She found the bill had all been paid,
And signed below (not camp or girly)
Was the name of Eddie Murphy

Untooth

Mr D'Arch the demon dentist
Was extreme in his depravity
But now he's found
Deep underground
He's filling his last cavity.

Vilerepugnantbitch

She talks in cruelty, like a blight
Of loudness, crimes and scary eyes,
And all that beast of darkened fight
Greet in her last spec and her lies,
Cuss yellowed zoo-cat renders fright
Stitch weaponed to gory play of knives.

One raid – the store, one stain, the mess,
Lad half impaled, the shameless face
Which prays for overt craven stress,
It's grimly spiteful on her face;
Her thoughts uncaring austere express,
Now lure you near their wanton space.

And what a cheek - 'Hand o'er that cow!!!!'
So knocked , so armed, set negligent,
She smirks (that grim,) the taunts that
grow,
But tell of days in Hola'way spent,
A kind that knees those all below,
A skank whose law is virulent.

Squirrelled Away

You may have met them,
I refer to the Somairni family
Formerly of Abu Dhabi
But now proprietor of a locally famous
Michelin star restaurant
In a converted farmhouse near Baxterley.
The chef Abdul Somairni.
In the game season Prepared stew for the
freezer
Using some skinned squirrels.
But mostly some plucked crows.
This proved fortuitous as on one occasion
A coach broke down on an adjacent meadow
Disgorging fifty very hungry prison inmates.
They having been travelling for six hours
And the coach driver having slavishly
followed his sat nav.
They raided the freezer
and The felons feasted.
And thus the occurrence was reported
In the local Newsrag
Concluding:

Never in a field of human convicts,
Was so much bowled,
By Somairni,
Via crow stew.

The job of clearing my aunt's house to my father was entrusted
after her sad departing

Absolutelytrilling

And in the guise of money's louse
An idea that after done and dusted.
Had the same amount when starting
He decided to contact her spirit
So to séance he departed
But no word from her transmitted,
But stretching credulity to the limit
The budgie pronounced open hearted
Where the tiny space the cash now fitted.

And I was told when six or seven
What the avian said was true
And as he did not refer, not ever
The rest is better left to you.

Cracking Up

Have you heard
the one about the drug pusher
who has been committed for a court appearance.
He will be hauled up at Stafford assizes,
in front of His Lordship Justice Derror.
The prosecution plan portray him
not as hero in the local community
but as a bit of a downer and outer.
The whole thing will be sorted out in time
one way or another by trial an' Derror.

Misvisage

I was in my office
having just visited
The Isle of Dogs, Eastend,
Reviewing the winners
Of the regional heats of
Grotesque face Golden Gob awards.
(A sort of Miss World of the gargoyles)
In preparation for the finals.
England South East had
produced an interesting tied result
i.e. The Minner twins: Harold and Albert
Who were actually not related.
Having printed and cropped
One example of each of the contestants'
most contorted faces,
They were now staring out from my notice board
As I pondered:
Minner 'nd Minner, on the wall
Who is the scariest of Millwall

The Haggis roams the Highland – minus kilt.

The Fragrant Haggis

The haggis heard is rarely found
Like a weir wolf that's not musical,
Others say it's like the sound
Inside a gents loo cubicle.

Very few have ever seen one,
But some have joined the Club,
Which may explain
Why it's seen again (and again!)
On the way back from the pub.

They have families five or six
For haggis are like rats,
That's why a father gave his kids
Their own cricket bats.

It has a reclusive lifespan
Becomes aggressive if you pry,
They know hunters stalk the hills
You'll regret it if you try.

You can visit a Scot's festival
To the 'Chippy' taxi ride,
You'll find it indigestible
When battered and deep fried.

A haggis taste on Flame's Night
Will feed the hungry man,
And he'll say what he's thankful for
It doesn't taste like spam.

Frank, an avid Wolverhampton Wanderers supporter,
ruminates over club relegation during Sunday lunch.

Wolfitdown

When to the sessions of streaked Sunday pork
I suppon up the o'er'ndulgence of things mashed,
I cite the stack of many a thing I forked,
And o'er fold toes, bewail my beer primed waist:
When can I down a pint? (Much used to flow,
With specious friends hid in W'therspoons last night,)
And heap afresh Wolves wronged grim-stantial woe,
And moan the defence of many a clannish fight:
Then can I peeve as grievances tear on,
And heavily from moan to moan tell o'er
The mad account on footy-loaded groan,
Which by now played (and will not aid the score.)
But if the while I think on season's end,
All losses are restored if fixtures mend.

Authorplusmushrooms

The publisher looked at my book text
Hoping to make cash that's hard.
He inferred that my poems would look good
Next to Milton or to Poe or the Bard.

(At first I couldn't get why he was comparing my
work to disinfectant or a chamber pot – well might
have a point there, or what I was barred from.
I did not see this one coming
I give things some thought that's my rule
I thought ,'This is plain money grubbing'
He had me down for a fool. (as if!)

155

'Your verse would outshine Merry Shelley
The one who sells on the sea-shore
You must want to join the great poets
Your work would look good there I'm sure.'

Waking my wife – a voice screamed
in my head
But all the great poets are dead.'

**As pictured in the superb film 'Young
Frankenstein'**

At the height of the thunderstorm
Dr. Frankenstein and the monster
are hoisted heavenwards amid the tumult.
The monster metal overstrapped on the gurney.

The lightning thunderbolts crash
menacingly on all sides.
The noise is ceaseless and majestic
causing all who witness to marvel
at this primal feast of latent power.

Thunderbolts hurtle exploding in cascades of sparks
igniting the electrodes,
Lighting the monster's face as if his
Inner luminescence was being summoned.
Almost unnoticed from the monster's mouth
a crimson emission secretes and drains
creepily toward the earth.
Dr. Frankenstein now enthused to the point
of incontinence proceeds to bellow –
'IT'S SALIVA! (repeatedly)'

Night out

'Quarkdom of Skin-Freaks'
Was not only the first 007/Zombie film ever made,
but probably the last.
I had been dragged along to our local fleapit by
Maggy, my partner.
A good sort but a bit of an alchy.
She always snook in cans of Extra Strength Lager in
her handbag,
Which I judiciously refused.
'Oh go on, you know you want to,'
She propositioned me,
But no way.
I can see it now
– being stopped on the way home
(Slurred voice – police siren)
'Good Consternoon Afterble'
I can hear the cell door closing....

Back at the Multisex –
Gratuitous violence,
hacked off tree limbs
and gory mondeos filled the screen.

It weren't my cuppa tea,
But then those of the visceral enlightenment filling
the other seats,
should be getting their money's worth.
Well that's what I reckoned,
No I never did like creepy films
since that day I saw Pinochio
turn into a pizzahouse.

But I sat there all the same
'Cause I was hoping for a little favour later...
(James Blond gives blokes ideas)
Anyway it didn't seem long 'til we were leaving and
that's when it occurred to me while passing the
hamster food counter,
that I was feeling as you might expect,
Like the 007 gulpdown shaken – but not slurred.

.

King Tut (can't in nude)

A room came next with table laid
Hot soup in a great big cup
The prof dipped and licked his finger
And that's when I threw up

The walls where murals colour roared
With royals and good people
And Tut in boat was looking bored
His pet a huge dung beetle

One worker he took some gold
And went to cross the Nile
He tried to move a large green log
He was eaten by a crocodile.

Some Arab ladies came to us
We heard a lot of laughter
What do you sphinx? Just drink tea!
They always liked to natter.

The prof and I we picked up
Some empty jars. No chance!

I put them in my pocket and got
Ants inside my pants
They said there was a curse on us
That's twitter you'd agree
Then my camel ate my sandwiches
So we scarpered for GB.

Ode To Those Four-Letter Words

Banish the use of those four-letter words
Whose meanings are never obscure.
The Angles and Saxons, those bawdy old birds,
Were vulgar, obscene and impure.
But cherish the use of the weak-kneed phrase
That never quite says what you mean;
For better you stick to your hypocrite ways
Than be vulgar, or coarse, or obscene.

When Nature is calling, plain-speaking is out,
When ladies, God bless 'em, are milling about,
You make water, wee-wee, or empty the glass;
You can powder your nose, 'Excuse me' may pass;
Shake the dew off the lily, see a man 'bout a dog;
Or when everyone's soused, it's condensing the fog,
But be pleased to consider and remember just this –
That only in Shakespeare do characters ****!

You may speak of a movement, or sit on a seat,
Have a passage, or stool, or simply excrete;
Then groan in pure joy in that smelly old shack.
You can go lay a cable, or do number two,
Or sit on the toidy and make a do-do,
Or say to the others, 'I'm going out back',

But ladies and men who are socially fit
Under no provocation will go take a ****!

When your dinners are hearty with onions and
beans,
With garlic and claret and bacon and greens; Your
bowels get so busy distilling a gas
That Nature insists you permit it to pass.
You are very polite and you try to exhale Without
noise or odour – you frequently fail –
Expecting a zephyr, you carefully start,
But even a deaf one would call it a ****!

A woman has bosoms, a bust or a breast. Those lily-
white swellings that bulge 'neath her vest;,
They are towers of ivory, sheaves of new wheat;
In a moment of passion, ripe apples to eat.
You may speak of her nipples as small rings of fire
With hardly a question of raising her ire;
But by Rabelais' beard, she'll throw fifteen fits
If you speak of them roundly as good honest
****.

Banish the use of those four-letter words
Whose meanings are never obscure.
The Angles and Saxons, those bawdy old birds,
Were vulgar, obscene and impure.
But cherish the use of the weak-kneed phrase
That never quite says what you mean;
For better you stick to your hypocrite ways
Than be vulgar, or coarse, or obscene.

ALOTBSOL

For the music at the crem
He wanted something daft
He wanted 'Wake me up'
So his mates could have a laugh.

And as the curtains closed
There was to be a surprise
He wanted them to all join in with
'Smoke gets in your eyes'

Awaywithwords

Two more row, and too follow and to swallow.
Neeped this pretty plaice from gravy say
To the vast grillable of afforded thyme.
And haul of chef's days have blighted drools
(The wait drew Trusty Beth.)
Out, shout leek scandal.
Th'wife's butter forking yellow, on floor greyer.
Then chucks and rests her flour upon the sage
And then is curd no more. Bit in a stale
Roll by itinerants, full for browned off brew'y -
Signal; Defying huffing.

Chickenrunend

The old question that's never been solved
The egg preceded but wasn't the chicken involved
But has the answer-come (We've not rehearsed)
Send off to Amazon
And see which one comes first.

Around here they call me 'Top Dog'

Alapineohish

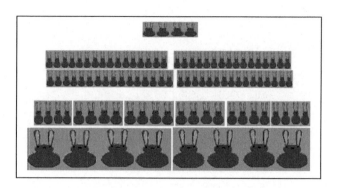

The Bunnying of Napoleon

The peace treaty now the French had signed
As did the Russians (top-dog blind?)
Napoleon's ascent was at its height
Where next would he choose to bite?

All finalised with Russian nation
And Royals and those represented
(Now faced an unknown lapine legation)
A rabbit hunt for high of station.

Napoleon was now on site
Positioned in full view
He stood apart
He scarcely moved
Though all at once could tell
He had no need of elitist cliques
(But was only five foot six)
He motioned to indicate, a sign
That those to who long had stood in line
To let loose, released en mass,
The harmless creatures now at last.

164

Huge numbers then escaped the clasp
Of make-shift hutch, damp ditch or grasp
Instead of leaving to afford a chase
They then toward Napoleon raced
And soon their presence didn't beg
Then climbed right up his bony legs.

And Napoleon without a shout
With tens and hundreds round about
He swiped them off oft' arms aloft
And they with twisted legs and necks.
They didn't know what happened next.

As loss seemed very close at hand
Caught unprepared to make a stand
(A thousand Bigwigs out of hand)
And like his battle foes elite
He opted for a quick retreat
And in a move somewhat disgraced
In ire, to his carriage he made haste.

And many after did relate
Those timid creatures frenzied state,
Caused them the initiative to gain
(Who doubts seeing or can explain?)
Acted as if in army ranks
Divided in two ordered flanks
Which attempted to outrun with pep
To gain first, the carriage step.

A few long eared cotton tails
By dint of agile speed entails
The coach's open mouth sucked in

On seats for VIP's within
By a hare's breath lay in wait
They'd have to pay their coach fare late.

But there was risk
For Napoleon having none of this
He shut the door
and made short work of those aboard.

He gave them all a Concorde rite.
Their first experience of flight.
For out the window all he threw
Even those that in someone's view
Could make decent rabbit stew.

(They'd need a three star chef with spleen
To make a fragrant hors cuisine.
And piling more of hour by hour
Could represent the Eiffel Tower.)

So honour was restored at last
On which Napoleon refused to dwell
It was one day's minor blot
(Though Wikipedia they knew not!)
As likely soon would be forgot.

There was no question
He was a mighty warrior who had quelled
Such fight-forces that befell
In instances of plan ahead
Or react fast or take as read.
But jawst a thought
As you may think - I'll say

No one of class would e'er refur
In crass thump-ground way
To that (excruciating) bad hare day.
A way he couldn't ever find
To keep the funny side in mind
For thinking thus he had good reason-
It was defeat by bunny legion.

Meet the Hoodys

Robin, Will and Johners
were members of the Hoody family.
Maybe you've heard of them
They're famous because they have
an arboreal interest bordering on mania.
Trees fill the lives of these reprobates
Though tree fellers they are not.
Robin is the most recognisable
He's the one with a bow.... In his hair.

Every day rising early at 11am
they (being peckish)
visit the Friar Truck
(the proprietor being no less than
Omaha Sherriff formerly of Snottingham)
for a bacon sandwich-hazel baguette
Before proceeding to the local forest
With their chipper mate Douglas Fir
Who is often axed along.

Poor Johners (the elder of the three) looks sad,
Having been jilted at the altar by his sick amour,
she left him in the larch pining away.

Life can certainly deal you a poor hand.
Somewhat in reverse
Robin's seen a little too much
of his lady love recently
with her 24/7 last week
(You could say he's a little maid marionated.)

In t'woodland archery features now
And after a harrowing target practise
They proceed to carve 'Acorns rule, Oak eh?'
In plane English for all to see.
Except they chose the nearest beech.

A little burglary may follow
A certain vile tongued virago's house
Was the last one.
Though they give most of the proceeds
to a German charity thus - robbing the witch
To give to the Ruhr.

It's a fact that Robin aspires
to become a follower of
A secular society-brotherhood - The Menin.

He fancies dressing in the vermin robes
undergoing some farcical initiation ritual
before being ordained
into the lower order of the Menintites.

They finish their day
And I wont palm you off
In front of the box.
Would that I could leaf it alone.

Manysicked Slumbercatch

Before we were married Chris (short for Christine) and I went on a holiday to Sweden . We travelled in my battered old mini to Newcastle upon Tyne and had a pleasant 'flat as a millpond' sea-crossing of about 24 hours to Gothenburg.

The holiday was largely uneventful. We camped and walked and visited Oslo by train, where food was quite expensive. I do remember one morning when we woke to a kind of zipping sound going down the side of the tent. This turned out to be the local small birds which were perching on the apex of the tent and then sliding down the fabric and having a great time. We also saw two ten year old girls in swimming costumes playing on a slide in about 18" of water, in a lake, splashing around and having a lot of fun. Thinking it a good idea we ventured in only to find the water to be near freezing point. (Note: Swedish ladies are no wimps.)

On the last day we needed to return to Gothenburg but found that the car wouldn't start. This was probably due to the 'headlights on' Swedish law. So, needing a push we asked some burly Swedish campers for help. They positively enjoyed the experience and shouted to each other happily.

As the car started, one of them yelled 'Fromstat' and the others all cheered. (Apparently this meant 'flying start.')

As we neared Gothenburg I realised that we were running out of fuel which I promptly forgot about until the engine died on the quayside. I departed with the water container to buy fuel leaving Chris wondering what would happen if the queue started to embark. Luckily I was back in time. On board the ferry all went well except that I managed to irreparably break my glasses – something that was to prove unhelpful later on.

At about 3am that night the weather deteriorated somewhat. Probably about a force 4 – 5 gale resulting in much rolling. I don't know if you have experienced a sea journey like this one but if you haven't then perhaps I could explain a little – the ship rolls (as you face the bows ie. the way the ship is travelling) from right to left, at the same time as it climbs waves it rolls from front to rear. Rolling also takes place on either diagonal sometimes veering unpredictably from one to the other. Combine all three and the result of this was fairly obvious for a couple of landlubbers like Chris and myself. Heave ho.

Inside the cabin strange things began to occur – the bunk bed (hinged down the long side) that I had recently vacated began to move up and down of its own accord. At the time this mystified me but I soon realised that we have this built in perception that the 'walls don't move' which meant that to my mind the walls were always vertical, thus a bed that behaved in this way was decidedly odd

Now we became very seasick and decided to leave the cabin. Someone advised us to move down to the lower decks where the motion of the boat was less but this didn't help so we climbed to the passenger deck level where the fresh air and being able to see the horizon did make a small difference. We stayed there for the rest of the night talking to other passengers and looking forward to being on dry land again.

Some hours later we were summoned to the car deck to disembark only to find that the car was still

refusing to behave itself - so Chris got out and we both pushed the mini towards a ramp, on which I bump started the engine. The ramp had a 'No Walking ' sign on it, but a member of the ship's crew, with something of a belittling look, gave Chris the nod to carry on and run down it to catch up.

On dry land again we decided not to camp but instead to go for a B & B where I had the oddest sensation whist walking up the staircase – the steps and walls moved as if I was still on the ship. In the room we were soon bedded down in two single beds, feeling grateful to be back safely on land we were very soon asleep.

The next thing I remember was having a worrying dream that I was back on board. Half sleepwalking I made for the door, was through it and on the landing hearing the lock snap closed behind me before I realised what I was doing. Fortunately I was wearing pyjamas.

Now slightly disorientated I wasn't absolutely sure which room I'd come from. Trying the door to the right I found it was open and walking in found a stranger, fortunately fast asleep, in my bed. Oops wrong room. Exit stage left pronto. Now certain which room I needed I decided to go downstairs. Just then another resident came up the stairs. I don't remember what I said to him but he went away with a rather surprised look on his face

Heading downstairs feeling my way down a dark corridor I reached into a side room and flipped on a light switch. Almost at my feet there appeared a small dog, lying on its back, tongue hanging out fortunately totally relaxed. It then occurred to me that I would probably give the lady owner a heart attack if I carried on, so with the brain finally working I decided to ring the front door bell. Chris was still asleep as I was readmitted to the room.

Next morning over breakfast the lady owner asked us if we'd slept well - to which the reply was – yes eventually. Two days or so later we arrived home where Chris's father commented that both of us still looked green.

From 'Verse and Worse'
No copyright issues and suitable, when
copied, at your discretion, for all ages.

Manners

I eat my peas with honey;
I've done it all my life.
It makes the peas taste funny,
But it keeps 'em on the knife.

Longing

I wish I was a little grub
With whiskers round my tummy,
I'd climb into a honey-pot
And make my tummy gummy.

Ware Tomato-Juice

An accident happened to my brother Jim
When somebody threw a tomato at him –
Tomatoes are juicy and don't hurt the skin,
But this one was specially packed in a tin.

Manners

There was a young lady of Tottenham,
Who had no manners or else she'd
forgotten 'em;
At tea at the vicars
She whipped off her knickers
Because, she explained, she felt 'ot in 'em.

The Rash Lady of Ryde

There was an old lady of Ryde
Who ate some green apples, and died.
The apples, (fermented inside the
lamented)
And made cider inside her inside.

The Irish Pig

'Twas an evening in November,
As I very well remember,
I was strolling down the street in drunken
pride, But my knees were all a'flutter
So I landed in the gutter,
And a pig came up and lay down by my side.

Yes, I lay there in the gutter
Thinking thoughts I could not utter,
When a colleen passing by did softly say,
'Ye can tell a man who boozes
By the company he chooses' —
At that, the pig got up and walked away!

Hodge's Grace

Bless us heavenly father
And keep us all alive
There's ten of us for dinner
And not enough for five.

The Young Lady of Riga,

There was a young lady of Riga,
Who rode, with a smile, on a tiger.
They returned from the ride
With the lady inside
And the smile on the face of the tiger.

The Replete Pelican

A funny old bird is a pelican.
His beak can hold more than his belican.
Food for a week
He can hold in his beak,
But I don't know how the helican.
Dixon Lanier Merritt

PailintoInsignificance

There was an old man of Nantucket
Who kept all his cash in a bucket,
But his daughter, named Nan,
Ran away with a man,
And as for the bucket, Nantucket.

Rumbletum

I sat next to the duchess at tea;
It was just as I feared it would be:
Her rumblings abdominal
Were truly phenomenal,
And everyone thought it was me!
Pres. Woodrow Wilson?

John Bunn

Here lies John Bunn,
He was killed by a gun.
His name was not Bunn, but Wood,
But Wood would not rhyme with Gun,
But Bunn would.

The Old Lady of Ryde

There was an old lady of Ryde
Who ate some green apples and died.
The apples fermented inside the lamented
And made cider inside her inside

Kickedthebucket?

Doctor Bell fell down a well
And broke his collar bone
Doctors should attend the sick
And leave the well alone.

IQWordplay

Beneath this smooth stone,
By the bone of his bone,
Sleeps Mr Jonathan Gill.
By lies when alive
This attorney did thrive,
And now that he's dead he lies still.

*I remember Spike Milligan
reciting this limerick on TV*

There was an old man from Darjeeling,
Who travelled from London to Ealing
It said on the door,
'Please do not spit on the floor'
So he carefully spat on the ceiling.

Here I learned a little about accents

The Budding Bronx
(The Bronx, New York)

Der spring is sprung
Der grass is riz
I wonder where den boidies is?

Der little boids is on der wing,
Ain't dat absoid?
Der little wings is on the boid.

Slightlyaltered

There was an old fellow from Lyme
Who married three wives at one time;
When asked: 'Why the third?'
He replied, 'One's absurd;
And bigamy, Sir, is a crime.'

Upstartitis

'Tis dogs delight to bark and bite
And little girls to sing.
And if you sit on a red hot brick
It's the sign of an early spring.

Theorydamage

There was a young lady named Bright
Whose speed was far faster than light;
She went out one day,
In a relative way,
And returned on the previous night.

Amphibiana

What a wonderful bird the frog are
When he stand he sit almost
When he hop, he fly almost
He ain't got no sense hardly;
He ain't got tail hardly either.
When he sit, he sit on what he ain't got,

Limericks

'I'm glad pigs can't fly' said young Sellars,
(He was one of them worrying fellas)
'We know what pigs do in a sty
So if pigs they could fly
We'd all have to carry umbrellas.

The Bleedin' Sparrer

We 'ad a bleedin' Sparrer
Lived up the bleedin' spaht,
One day the bleedin' rain came down
An' washed the bleeder aht.

An as 'e layed 'arf drahned
Dahn in the bleedin' street
'E begged the bleedin' rainstorm
To have his bleedin'feet.

But then the bleedin'sun came out
Dried up the bleedin'rain
So the bleedin' sparrer
He climbed the spout again.

But, Oh! The bleedin' sparrer'awk
'e spies 'im in ' snuggery,
'Eere sharpens up 'is bleedin'claws
An' rips ' I'm out by thuggery!

Just then a bleedin 'sportin' type
Wot 'wot 'ad a bleedin' gun
'E spots the bleedin' sparrer 'awk
'An blasts 'is bleedin' fun

The moral of this story
Is plain for everyone
Them wot's up the bleedin 'spaht
Don't get no bleedin' fun. '

Mary

Mary had a little bear
To which she was so kind
And everywhere that Mary went
You saw her bear behind.
(With my own last line)

*The English have long been avid quaffers of
large quantities of beer and would enjoy a
good rhyme at the 'Jug and Bucket.'*

A Rhyme
Inscribed on Pint Pot

There are several reasons for drinking,
And one has just entered my head;
If a man cannot drink while he's living
How the hell can he drink when he's dead?

Doctor Bell

Doctor Bell fell down a well
And broke his collar bone
Doctors should attend the sick
And leave the well alone.

The Iron Curtain

On Nevski bridge a Russian stood
Chewing his beard through lack of food.
Said he, 'Tis tough stuff to eat
But a darn sight better than Shredded
wheat!'

Castaway

He grabbed me round my slender neck,
I could not shout or scream,
He carried me into his room
Where we could not be seen;
He tore away my flimsy wrap
And gazed upon my form

I was so cold and still and damp,
While he was wet and warm.
His feverish mouth he pressed to mine
— I let him have his way
He drained me of my very self,
I could not say him nay.
He made me what I am.
Alas! That's why you find me here...
A broken vessel, broken glass,
That once held bottled Beer.

Happy Nonsense

Twas in the month of Liverpool,
In the city of July,
The snow was raining heavily,
The streets were very dry,
The flowers were sweetly singing,
The birds were in full bloom,
As I went down to the cellar
To sweep the upstairs room

Happier Nonsense

One fine day in the middle of the night,
Two dead men got up to fight,
Back to back they faced each other,

Drew their swords and shot each
other.
One was blind and the other couldn't
see,
So they chose a dummy for a referee.
A blind man went to see fair play,
A dumb man went to shout "Hooray!"

A paralysed donkey passing by,
Kicked the blind man in the eye,
Knocked him through a nine inch wall,
Into a dry ditch and drowned them all,

A deaf policeman heard the noise,
And came to arrest the two red toys,
If you don't believe this story's true,
Ask the blind man he saw it too!

The years I spent as a primary school music teacher this song was always a success.

Football Crazy

I have a favourite brother,
And his Christian name is Paul.
He's lately joined a football club
For he's mad about football.
He's got two black eyes already
And teeth lost from his gob,
Since Paul became a member of
That terrible football club.

(Chorus) For he's football crazy,
He's football mad,
The football it has taken away
The little bit o' sense he had,
And it would take a dozen servants
To wash his clothes and scrub,
Since Paul became a member of
That terrible football club.

In the middle of the field, one afternoon,
The captain says, "Now Paul,
Would you kindly take this penalty-kick
Since you're mad about football?"
So he took forty paces backwards,
Shot off from the mark.

The ball went sailing over the bar
And landed in New Yark!
His wife, she says she'll leave him
If Paulie doesn't keep
Away from football kicking
At night-time in his sleep.
He calls out 'Pass, McGinty!"
And other things so droll
Last night he kicked her out of bed
And swore it was a goal!
(Chorus)
James Curran?

My thanks to Unsplash for excellent the images, and all who assisted me in the writing and compiling of this book.

The Author - Alan Joynson
mr.a.joynson@gmail.com

In women orgasms are different according to the
menstrual cycle. When not on her period waves form in
an inward direction assisting the sperm to swim at
speeds of up to 28 mph.

There was a young geezer called Harry-Pinne
Liked fast cars and football and dallyin'
But his girl got enthralled
About nothing at all
And that 'nothing at all?' - she just married him.

A recent Natural History TV programme using night
vision technology, showed a 'nubile' female rhino
feigning sleep to rid her of unwanted amorous
advances.

A male stripper at a hotel in the West Midlands, used a flame thrower as part of his act, causing fire alarms to be triggered and panic in the mainly female audience. To add to his woe he descended the popularity ladder the moment the fire brigade arrived and found themselves surrounded by hordes of excited women. A Fire Brigade spokesman said, 'The stripper didn't get a look in once the lads had arrived. I think it's something to do with the uniform.

Some people think that having large breasts makes a woman stupid. Actually it's quite the opposite, a woman having large breasts makes men stupid.
Rita Rudner

Women need a reason to have sex. Men just need a place.   Billy Crystal

Researchers at Oxford and Coventry universities have found elderly people who have regular sex have higher cognitive function than those who do not. (This is unrelated to the 'five a day campaign – though it's worth trying for.)

A lady met a man on her night out with the girls. She decided, probably after some intake of alcohol, to allow him to take her to his house where they ended up in bed together.
When she woke up late the following morning he had disappeared. She then heard footsteps on the stairs and shortly in walked an estate agent and his clients. She was somewhat shocked to find she had spent the night in a show-house.

By the same author

Garden Images using colour reverse for design projects - Amazon

The pictures in this book were taken with a moderately priced mobile phone using the colour reverse setting mostly in my own garden. (As on the cover – all greens become purple.)

There is no copyright which I hope will mean that someone can use these images for fabric design or some other creative project.

Printed in Great Britain
by Amazon